Kathleen's Shaken Dreams

BOOK ONE
of the
A Life of Faith: Kathleen McKenzie Series

TRACY LEININGER CRAVEN

MCP
Mission City Press

Franklin, Tennessee

Book One of the *A Life of Faith: Kathleen McKenzie* Series

Kathleen's Shaken Dreams
Copyright © 2006, Mission City Press, Inc. All Rights Reserved.

Published by Mission City Press, Inc.

Cover & Interior Design: Richmond & Williams
Cover Photography: Michelle Grisco Photography
Typesetting: BookSetters

For more information, write to Mission City Press at 202 Second Avenue South, Franklin, Tennessee 37064, or visit our Web Site at: **www.alifeoffaith.com.**

For a FREE catalog call 1-800-840-2641.

Library of Congress Catalog Card Number: 2006930435
Craven, Tracy Leininger
    Kathleen's Shaken Dreams
    Book One of the *A Life of Faith: Kathleen McKenzie* Series
    ISBN-13: 978-1-928749-25-7
    ISBN-10: 1-928749-25-9

Printed in the United States of America
  6 7 8 9 — 11 10 09

DEDICATION

To my husband, David, for his unfailing love and support and to our precious daughter Elaina Hope.

AMERICAN LIFE IN THE 1920S

*T*he era in which Kathleen McKenzie grew up is often referred to as the Roaring Twenties. The economy was booming and new inventions were being made daily. By the end of the 1920s, the majority of city homes were equipped with indoor plumbing and electricity. This enabled even the most common housing to have modern conveniences such as telephones, refrigerators, electric stoves, vacuum cleaners, washing machines, and perhaps most popular of all, the radio.

It was not only the bustling economy that dubbed the 1920s the Roaring Twenties. Unlike the decades before, there was a strong pursuit of personal entertainment. Many historians attribute this to the fact that people were willing to do almost anything for pleasure after the horrors of World War I, known as "The Great War." But whatever the case, the Broadway stage, radio, and silent movies were becoming quite the rage. Dancing and professional sports were also gaining popularity. More than ever before in history, radio and newspaper ads encouraged Americans to spend money on entertainment and modern conveniences. Because of the media and constant push for pleasure, many people view the Roaring Twenties as a decade of decadence and extravagance. For Kathleen, and the average American family, living was comfortable but not excessive. Entertainment involved activities such as attending a baseball game with the family or going to a church social.

THE STOCK MARKET AND THE CRASH

Much of the wealth that fueled the excesses of the Roaring Twenties was provided by the *stock market*—a place where people buy and sell *stocks*. Stocks are shares of ownership in a company. Because the economy had been so strong for over a decade, shares in many companies had enormously increased in value. Everyone knew people who had greatly profited from buying stocks, and that influenced them to invest their savings as well, further fueling the stock market. Even though they knew almost nothing about the company whose shares they bought, they believed that they could not lose. Everyone was making bushels of money in the stock market! Greed took over, and many people borrowed money from the bank to buy more stock. This created more demand and stock prices went higher. People borrowed more money, mortgaged their houses, farms, or businesses, and still stocks increased in value.

It seemed there would be no end to the profits—that is until the day the stock market crashed on Black Tuesday, October 29, 1929. The value of the stocks plunged so severely that it wiped out all of the investors' previous profits and they didn't have the money to pay back their loans to the bank. Many lost their homes, farms, and businesses. Their employees lost their jobs

and could not pay their home mortgages. Soon the banks failed, and even people who had never risked their savings on stocks lost everything.

As more businesses failed, more people lost their jobs, more banks failed, and more savings were wiped out, until it seemed that no one would survive the financial catastrophe.

THE PRICE OF LIVING IN KATHLEEN'S DAY

Seeing America's economy through the eyes of the 1920s is both fascinating and astonishing. In our modern world it is unlikely that we could walk into a department store and pay a dollar for a brand-new dress or go to the local cinema for ten cents. But in Kathleen's day, this was the normal cost of living, and during the Roaring Twenties thousands of consumers enjoyed spending their hard-earned cash. The following are some examples of prices in Kathleen's day.

THE PRICE OF LIVING:

Food

Apples	10 cents a pound
Bread	5 cents for a one-pound loaf
Corn	39 cents for 3 cans
Flour	4 cents a pound
Sugar	47 cents for 10 pounds
Pork and beans	25 cents for 3 cans
Ground hamburger	10 cents for one pound

Kathleen's Shaken Dreams

Clothing

Woman's dress	$1.00
Man's boots	$2.98
Sweater	$1.00
Jacket	$1.98
Overalls	$1.50

Car

Chevy sedan	$565.00
Chevy pickup	$440.00

Furniture and Appliances

Electric iron	$8.95
Vacuum cleaner	$30.00
Electric washer	$33.50
Radio	$69.50
Refrigerator	$99.50
Electric stove	$124.50

Extras and Entertainment

Private music lessons	$0.50 per lesson
Public swimming pool	$0.10
Theater (silent movie)	$0.10
Traveling circus	$0.25
Sled with steers	$3.95–8.95
Doll	$1.95

McKenzie Family Tree

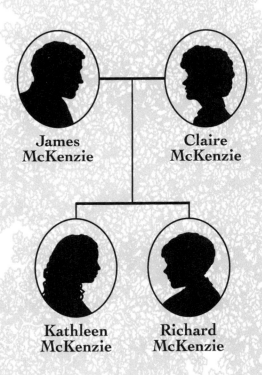

James
McKenzie

Claire
McKenzie

Kathleen
McKenzie

Richard
McKenzie

SETTING

$\mathcal{T}$he story begins in July 1929, in Fort Wayne, Indiana, on the morning of the Monroeville Fair and Highland Games.

CHARACTERS

 THE MCKENZIE HOUSEHOLD

James McKenzie — Age 35: Kathleen's father and head accountant for a major construction company in Fort Wayne, Indiana

Claire McKenzie — Age 32: Kathleen's mother
  Their children:
  Kathleen McKenzie — Age 11
  Richard McKenzie — Age 9

 OTHERS

Mr. and Mrs. Meier — A new family who recently moved to Fort Wayne with their children:

Lucy Meier — Age 12, Kathleen's new friend

Peter — Age 14

Rose — Age 16

Helen — Age 17

Deanna — Age 20

Dottie — Oldest sister, married

Reverend and Mrs. McCarthy — Pastor of Plymouth Congregationalist Church and his wife

Dr. and Mrs. Schmitt — Family doctor and his wife, friends of the McKenzies and parents of:

Freddie Schmitt — Schoolmate and friend of Kathleen

Miss Brooklin — Kathleen's language teacher

Miss Blake — Kathleen's history teacher

Patricia Barnett — Classmate, daughter of wealthy banker

Madelyn Barnett — Patricia's older sister, Kathleen's rival

Carrie — Classmate

Grace — Classmate

Jake — Neighborhood bully

Dan — Jake's sidekick

A Rude Awakening

*Your statutes are my heritage forever;
they are the joy of my heart.*

PSALM 119:111

"Good morning, Kathleen!" a familiar voice said. "It's time to wake up."

Kathleen McKenzie rubbed her eyes, squinted in the morning light, rolled over, and buried her face into her pillow. Her mind swirled in muddled and confused thought. *Where am I? Who is waking me up so early?*

"The sun won't stop rising just so . . ."

Kathleen barely heard the words. She yawned and drifted back to sleep.

"Did you hear what I said, lass? The sun won't stop rising just so our highland princess can catch her beauty sleep."

The words blended into Kathleen's dream . . .

The magnificent castle towered above the crest of an emerald peninsula that jutted out into the deep blue-green sea. On three

13

sides, thick, strong walls nestled on the edge of a cliff that fell hundreds of feet into the ocean below. On the fourth side, a deep, narrow gorge protected the castle from any enemy that might try to attack it. The drawbridge that spanned the gap was the only way into this impressive stone refuge. Gallant knights protected the princess who dwelled within.

On this particular day the princess and Kathleen ventured out of the castle to gather armfuls of fragrant heather and other wildflowers that grew in the fertile valley below, unaware of the danger that lurked in the shadows of the fortress. Only a few trusted knights knew of their whereabouts, and they were sworn to secrecy in order to protect the princess. There was suspicion of enemy spies within the castle walls.

Once their baskets were full, the carefree girls braided the flowers into garlands to grace their heads. When the sun was high in the sky, Kathleen returned to the castle to fetch a basket of food. The princess wanted to picnic along the banks of the rushing stream that leaped and tumbled its way over the rocky streambed as it raced through the valley to join the vast sea beyond.

Kathleen made her way up the steep hillside, stopping at the crest to catch her breath and admire the beauty of the lush valley and the brilliant ocean that stretched out before her. The deep blue sea looked as if the king had thrown all his diamonds into its depths and yet they sparkled as if determined not to be forgotten. Kathleen breathed deeply of the sweet-smelling salty sea air. In the distance she heard the lone cry of a seagull mixed with the crashing waves that surged against the rocky cliffs below.

A frightening, low-pitched moan broke into her dream.

A Rude Awakening

Kathleen's heart froze! The enemy was coming! Kathleen searched the horizon. Thirty warriors dressed in black with a red dragon on their chests and mounted on fierce steeds stood on the ridge above the lush valley where Kathleen had just left the princess. The princess was in great danger and did not know it — the sound of the rushing stream would drown out any warning signal! Kathleen had to do something. She raced back down the steep hill toward the valley. Time was short. She must rescue the princess.

The harsh noise grew from a low moan to a frightening high-pitched screech.

The enemy was closing in! Soon it would be too late!

Kathleen tossed and turned in her bed as the noise grew louder, groaning one moment and screeching dreadfully the next.

Finally the sound grew so loud it awoke Kathleen from her deep sleep. Startled, she sprang out of bed, sheets and blankets flying. Her wavy red hair fell wildly around her freckled face.

"The highland princess is in trouble!" she exclaimed. "We must save —"

The moan of Papa's bagpipes drifted up the stairs. Kathleen glanced about the room, trying to figure out where she was. Her gaze rested upon the pleasant, rosy-cheeked face of a woman with golden hair. It was her mother.

Mama's blue eyes shone with an amused twinkle. "Yes, my little princess?" She stooped over and gathered up Kathleen's bedding and a few stray feathers that had escaped from her pillow. "Is she in trouble? Or has she just had an adventurous dream?"

"Oh, Mama! It must have been a dream." Kathleen sat back on the bed and put her hand on her forehead. The bagpipes in the kitchen stopped, and Kathleen heard her father talking to Richard, her nine-year-old brother.

"Well, my laddie," Papa said in an exaggerated Scottish brogue, his voice so loud it carried clearly up the stairs into Kathleen's bedroom. "My bonnie old bagpipes from the motherland still work—even though they've been in the attic since last year's Highland Games!"

"The Highland Games!" Kathleen exclaimed. "How could I have forgotten?" Today was Saturday, the day of the Monroeville County Fair and Highland Games, and Kathleen had a million things to do to get ready. She jumped out of bed and threw her arms around her mother. "Good morning, Mama!" she said with a sudden burst of exuberance.

Mama lovingly patted her daughter on the back. "That's what I came to tell you. It is none other than the 27th of July, 1929—the day you have been waiting for all year. And, my dear princess, the sun is rising, and we still have to pack our picnic lunch, gather my preserves for the jams and jelly contest, and you have your homemade blueberry pie to box up for the dessert contest and—"

"And," Kathleen interrupted, "I still haven't finished hemming my doll dress for the junior sewing exhibit. Oh, Mama, I am excited beyond words, but . . ." Her

16

face sobered, and she put her hand over her stomach as if she were going to be ill. "I always get so nervous over the footraces. I know I won't be able to enjoy the fair until after the big race. What if I lose?"

"Don't be silly, Kathleen! Aren't you the one who just won first place in the Fort Wayne junior division of the citywide track meet?" Mama lifted Kathleen's chin and looked into her deep green eyes. "You always set such high goals for yourself, and that is good, but losing doesn't mean you're a failure."

"But, Mama, I'm only eleven and I'll be running with the twelve- and thirteen-year-olds because of where my birthday falls." Kathleen looked down at the floor. "What would Papa say if I lost?"

"Ahem!" Papa's tall, broad frame filled the doorway. Unlike Kathleen, Papa had dark brown hair and light brown eyes. His thin, distinguished mustache accentuated his broad smile. "I think your papa would say that he knows his daughter always gives her best. I think he'd be proud no matter what the outcome."

Mama nodded in agreement. "See, you have nothing to fret about. Now get up and get dressed while I finish making breakfast." She slipped out the door.

Kathleen looked up at Papa and wrinkled her brow. "Wouldn't you be a little disappointed if I lost?" Kathleen adored her papa and hated the thought of ever letting him down.

Papa put his hands on his daughter's shoulders and gave Kathleen a good-morning kiss on the top of her head, right where her stubborn cowlick parted her red hair. He was a gentle man who had a heart as big as his frame. No one would have guessed by his strong build and large hands that he was the head accountant for a major construction company in Fort Wayne, Indiana. Growing up on the family farm in Ohio had left its mark.

"Win or lose, I would much rather have a daughter who gave her all and finished strong than one who lost heart and gave up when the race got long and hard." Her father affectionately ran his finger down her lightly freckled nose. "You've given me a good idea for our morning devotional, my dear, so until then, don't think about —"

"Papa?" Richard stood in the doorway; his fine blond hair stuck up in every direction. "Do I really have to wear a skirt to the fair? Kathleen's kilt looks just like mine and I don't want to match my sister." He slumped his shoulders in despair and looked anxiously up at Papa. His big blue eyes resembled that of a puppy dog pleading for someone to come out and play. Kathleen tried not to laugh at the distraught look on her brother's flushed face.

"Why, my lad," Papa said using his strongest Scottish accent, "how will anyone know what clan you belong to? There won't be a Scottish man at the games that isn't proudly wearing a kilt. Some of the strongest, bravest men in history went to battle in a kilt just like the one you'll wear today."

"I know, Papa, but we are Americans, and I've never seen any of our soldiers in skirts before."

Kathleen turned her head to hide her grin and muffle a laugh. Mother always said that Richard might be small for his age, but there was nothing wrong with his brain.

Papa went to the door and swung Richard up to his shoulder.

"This is true, we are Americans — and proudly so for 364 days a year. But, once a year, at the Monroeville Highland Games, we celebrate our Scottish heritage. Son, you must never forget where you came from. It will help shape who you are." Papa strode down the hallway, carrying Richard with him. "There are many great, godly men that came before you and gave your clan a good name. There is nothing more important . . ."

Their words faded away as they entered Richard's room in search of the dreaded kilt.

Kathleen shut her bedroom door. The first bright rays of morning light streamed through the large window behind her bed, and outside the birds sang in the large oak tree. Kathleen opened the window, and the dewy fragrance from the lilac tree near her window filled her senses.

It was going to be a beautiful day. Her heart felt as if it would burst with excitement and anticipation as she hurriedly dressed for breakfast.

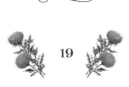

19

Kathleen's Shaken Dreams

"Breakfast was wonderful, my bonnie bride." Papa squeezed his wife's hand. "Nothing beats bacon, eggs, and a stack of hotcakes smothered in your homemade blackberry jam."

Kathleen ate hurriedly, excused herself from the table, and rushed back to her room to get her Bible. She settled on the living room sofa for family devotions. Mama played "Blessed Assurance" on the piano, and they all sang the first stanza. Kathleen loved to sing, but many times had to keep from laughing as the family tried to blend their voices in song. Papa and Richard sang out with all their hearts, but often in their enthusiasm, they sang off-key.

Papa opened his Bible and started reading from Hebrews chapter 12. "Therefore, since we are surrounded by such a great cloud of witnesses, let us throw off everything that hinders and the sin that so easily entangles, and let us run with perseverance the race marked out for us."

The race! Kathleen's heart jumped, and breakfast didn't seem to settle so well in her stomach. She had forgotten her anxiety in the busyness of the morning, but now it returned stronger than ever.

Maybe Papa and Mama would still be proud of her if she lost, but could she handle it? It was not that she had never lost before—she'd never even come close to winning the baking contest, and last year her sewing project had placed third. But for as long as she could remember, she had won the running events. Could she

lose a footrace without feeling like a failure? Could she lose and have the same positive attitude as if she'd won?

"You see, Kathleen," Papa said, looking up from his reading, "running footraces was popular even in biblical times."

Kathleen sat up straighter, embarrassed that Papa had caught her with her mind wandering.

"The passage I have just read says to set aside or throw off every hindrance that keeps us from running the race before us. Of course the apostle Paul is talking about the race of life, but I think it would help you to remember that today as you run. Try putting aside fear, pride, and discouragement—anything that could hinder you from running a good race and persevering to the end. Don't forget that you are to be an example of Christ in all you do."

"And don't forget you are representing our clan," Richard said.

"That's the spirit." Papa chuckled and tousled Richard's hair. "The McKenzie motto is *Luceo non Uro*— 'we shine, not burn.' Our goal should not be a burning desire to draw attention to ourselves in order to be revered like Christ. Instead we should strive to shine— reflecting His love and joy in everything we do. So go out there and run your best. Whatever happens, don't let your light go dim beneath a veil of fear, pride, or worry."

Kathleen nodded solemnly. She knew Papa was right—worry and fear would drain the energy and focus that she must apply to the race.

21

The Highland Games

Let your light shine before men, that they may see your good deeds and praise your Father in heaven.

MATTHEW 5:16

Kathleen took a deep breath and looked around. The fairgrounds, a large field at the edge of town that a local Scotsman donated each summer for the games, were strewn with countless white tents flapping in the early afternoon breeze. People were everywhere. The air was filled with sounds of laughter, the lively hum of Scottish bagpipes, and the occasional hoarse moo of a Highland cow.

"Look, Richard!" Kathleen laughed as she pointed at a pen with a shaggy cow whose long red hair hung like a mop about his face, hindering him from clearly viewing his curious spectators. "The poor creature's moo is almost as pitiful as his looks."

They had just finished a delicious picnic lunch with their parents and now they were free to explore the fairgrounds. Kathleen had won all the short sprints earlier that morning. This helped lighten her spirits a bit, but she would not be completely at ease until after her favorite race, the 440-yard sprint. The longer races were normally later in the day, which made Kathleen nervous because there were usually more spectators. But for now, she forced herself not to think about it. After all, there was so much to see and do before then.

"See, Richard, Papa was right; there are a lot of strong, confident men walking around clad in kilts." Kathleen pointed to a group of men who were passing by. In the middle of them was a tall, burly man who looked like a football player.

"They look pretty girly to me," Richard shrugged.

Kathleen ignored his comment. She enjoyed observing the different families walking about, each wearing their own tartan. You could pick a whole clan out of the crowd—from the little tykes to the grandpas—just by the colors they were wearing. There were all sorts of plaids arranged in a rich array of colors. Some tartans were predominately bright red, others blue, some deep burgundy, while still others a cheery yellow.

Kathleen looked down at her own kilt and smiled. "I like the McKenzie tartan the best." The vivid green, purple, and black check with a crisp, thin white line looked distinguished to Kathleen and she was proud to wear her clan's colors. "Didn't Papa look handsome with his full pipers plaid wrapped around his broad

chest and draped over his shoulder when he played in the band?"

"I suppose." Richard kicked at a clump of grass. "But I still don't see why strong men like Papa want to wear skirts."

Kathleen glanced around. How could she make Richard understand? She noticed some men across the field warming up for the tossing of the caber. She grabbed Richard's hand. "Come, I'll show you."

Kathleen led Richard to where some men dressed in kilts were picking up logs as thick and tall as telephone poles. "See that?" she said. "Those are called cabers."

They watched as a man, shorter than Papa, picked up a pole, cradled it in his cupped hands, and balanced the pole until it stood perpendicular on end.

"Wow," said Richard.

"That pole weighs well over a hundred pounds," explained Kathleen.

The man struggled toward a line drawn on the grassy field. With a great heave and loud groan, he threw it into the air, sending the caber toppling end-over-end. It landed with a thud, making a deep imprint in the soft dirt.

"How did he do that?" Richard exclaimed in awe.

"I think it has something to do with that kilt he's wearing."

Richard's mouth dropped open and he glanced down at his own garment, a new respect on his face.

Kathleen shook her head in amazement as the next contestant took his place.

"Let's go find out what time the tatty-sack competition is." Kathleen took Richard's hand and made her way through the crowd of bystanders. Besides the footraces, the tatty-sack war was about the only athletic contest for young boys. Kathleen loved to watch Richard, armed with a burlap bag full of cotton, wrap his legs tightly around a thin round fence post and hang on for dear life as he and the boy opposite him tried to knock each other off with their stuffed pillows. Kathleen sighed. It looked like such a challenge — but girls weren't allowed to participate. Her mama always said it would not be a very ladylike thing to do in public.

Kathleen chided herself. She had nothing to complain about. So far the day had been full of adventures and nothing but a success for the McKenzie family. Papa's bagpipes had resounded in rich bellows as he marched in the parade and then merrily piped reels and jigs for the Highland dance contestants. Mama's strawberry jam had won first prize at the county fair, and Kathleen's cooking and sewing skills seemed to have improved over the past year. Her little yellow and white doll outfit, with its matching ruffled pinafore, won honorable mention, and much to Kathleen's astonishment, her blueberry pie placed first. Papa was so proud of her that he couldn't stop telling all their friends and neighbors about it. Kathleen's outgoing personality didn't generally yield itself to shyness or embarrassment, but when it came to other people praising her, Kathleen's rosy cheeks deepened to a rich crimson color.

"Look, Kathleen!" Richard said as they neared the fence posts where the tatty-sack competition would take place. He pointed toward a shorter, balding man. "There's Dr. Schmitt, and Freddie is with him." Richard raised his eyebrows and smiled knowingly at Kathleen as he mentioned Freddie's name.

Kathleen's cheeks grew warm. She and Freddie had been good friends since first grade, and she was often teased about him. But Kathleen refused to believe the gossip that he had a crush on her. To her he was just a friend. Besides, she thought it was silly for girls her age to daydream about boys. Yet, despite this, she felt nervous whenever he was around. Kathleen's hands grew clammy as she followed Richard through the crowd toward Dr. Schmitt and Freddie.

Dr. Schmitt was not only their family doctor but also Papa's good friend. He was a jolly, kindhearted man with a laugh as large as his round belly. Some might think he would frighten his young patients with his big bushy eyebrows that accentuated the rather large balding spot in the middle of his head. Freddie's outgoing personality was like that of his father, but his facial features, wealth of curly brown hair, and tall, slender frame resembled his mother's side of the family.

"Dr. Schmitt, guess what!" Richard exclaimed as soon as he was in earshot. "Kathleen made a blue ribbon pie and got a big fat blueberry for it."

Both Dr. Schmitt and Freddie burst into laughter. Richard grinned from ear to ear, thoroughly satisfied with the attention. Ever since his Grandma McKenzie had told him about her old friend Miss Wealthy Stanhope, who would often confuse her words by accident, Richard decided that he would try it out just to be funny.

"You must mean your sister won a big, fat blue ribbon for her blueberry pie," Freddie said, glancing sideways at Kathleen, his eyes full of admiration.

Kathleen's cheeks burned with embarrassment.

"Attention! Attention!" someone called through a megaphone. "All 440-yard race contestants report to the starting line."

Kathleen's heart froze. That was her race. She glanced toward the field where the footraces were held and then back at Freddie and tried to act calm.

"Yes—yes, you're right. I don't know what Richard was talking about. It was my doll dress pie that got the . . . yellow ribbon." Despite her effort to remain composed, her words blurted out.

Richard looked up at her with a half-shocked, half-amused expression, and Freddie raised one eyebrow. Suddenly, Kathleen realized what she had said.

"Oh, goodness! What I was trying to say . . ." Kathleen backed toward the starting line.

"Attention! This is the last call for the 440 race."

"That's my race! I have to go. We're meeting my parents at the starting line." She turned and fled.

Kathleen's Shaken Dreams

"I'll be cheering for you," Freddie called after her.

Kathleen thought about how pleased he seemed with their brief visit, and it made the butterflies in her stomach even worse. Freddie was just being nice, she rationalized. There was no reason to imagine that he liked her any more than any other girl. Besides, she had to think about her race.

"There you two are," said Mama. "Richard, did you enjoy the tour of the fairgrounds with your sister?" Mama asked with her hands on her hips, almost as if she anticipated Richard having gotten into some sort of mischief. Richard nodded with a slightly guilty expression.

"Papa should be here soon." Mama handed Kathleen her shoes. "He ran into our banker, Mr. Barnett, and they got to talking about the recent rise in the stock market and the strong economy." She helped Kathleen unbuckle her kilt. "Kathleen, you'll have to hurry; your age group will be right after the ten and eleven-year-olds."

Underneath her kilt, Kathleen had worn her athletic knickers. Two layers were hot in the summer sun, but changing facilities at the makeshift fairgrounds were nonexistent.

Kathleen frowned at her knickers. They looked more like black bloomers than anything else. They extended below her knees and if she didn't do something about them they would slow her down. She eased the elastic cuffs above her knees to a more comfortable position. Her hands trembled as she tied her shoelaces in double knots.

28

"Just keep breathing," Kathleen whispered to herself. "Breathe in . . . go out there and run your hardest . . . breathe out . . . all that really matters is that you do your best."

"Are you nervous?" a girl standing nearby asked. She had a slight German accent. She was a short, delicate-looking girl with blonde hair, large blue eyes, and a pleasant smile.

The question surprised Kathleen. She had been so focused on winning the race that she hadn't even thought about politely conversing with the other competitors. Kathleen paused for a moment and then let out a little laugh.

"Yes, I always get nervous. How about you?"

"I guess I should be. This will be my first race — but my brother tells me I'm the fastest girl he has ever seen." The girl shrugged nonchalantly and her thoughts appeared to trail off. The next moment her bright smile returned. "My brother has always dreamed of competing in a Highland Games footrace like the great Scottish Olympic gold medalist, Eric Liddell. Anyway, Peter couldn't be here today, so I'm running this race especially for him." Once again, the girl's eyes got a faraway look.

Kathleen studied this new girl closely. She didn't look like an athlete, but there was something about her that made Kathleen want to know her better.

"All junior girl contestants to the starting line. That's right; we'll have all our twelve and thirteen-year-old

athletes to the line." The announcer shouted into his handheld megaphone, waving his arm over his head with exaggerated enthusiasm.

"We had better go. What did you say your name is?" Kathleen looked back, but the new girl had disappeared. Kathleen scanned the bystanders. She spied Papa's face—just enough of it to see him mouth that he'd be cheering for her. Kathleen waved nervously in reply. Then she made her way through the crowd and stepped over the rope separating the makeshift track from the rest of the field. Her legs felt like jelly as she walked to the starting line.

"Runners," said the man with the megaphone, "please organize yourselves from the inside lane out as I call your name and number."

Kathleen quickly glanced at the other contestants. There must be thirteen—no, fourteen other competitors. Most of the girls she recognized from last year, with the exception of a few new ones. Kathleen was tall for her age, but she felt short among these older girls. A couple of them looked her way. They seemed confident. Kathleen swallowed and then straightened her shoulders. She heard a few of the girls giggle and nod in her direction. Madelyn Barnett was among them. She was a wealthy girl from school and seemed to be too focused on herself to think of being kind to those around her. She smirked in Kathleen's direction and said something that made the girls standing next to her laugh. Kathleen tried to ignore them. She must

stay focused. If she got caught up in what Madelyn was doing, she'd lose.

"Kathleen McKenzie. Runner number 104." Kathleen caught her breath and numbly walked toward the announcer.

"That's right, little lady. You'll be right here on the inside lane." He looked at his list. "And next, we have Lucy Meier, number 215."

Lucy Meier! It was the girl with the German accent. She'd have to remember that name.

Lucy boldly marched up beside Kathleen. "Still nervous?" Lucy asked, as the announcer called out the rest of the names.

"Yes — quite." Kathleen's smile felt shaky.

"Runners, to your marks."

Every muscle in Kathleen's body tensed as she crouched into the starting position. She fixed her eyes straight ahead.

"Silence!" the announcer shouted, waving his starting gun in the air. The bagpipes at center field stopped playing their jig and the dance competitors paused. A hush fell over the crowd as they fixed their eyes on the starting gun.

"Get set."

Kathleen's stomach tightened and her heart pulsed with increasing speed.

Bang!

Kathleen sprang to her feet and sprinted toward the first curve. Because the racers were staggered at the

starting line and she was on the inside lane, Kathleen couldn't tell if she was ahead. But quick starts were her strength. Kathleen rounded the first curve and started down the straightaway. She glanced to the side. She was leading the pack!

Now if she could just maintain her lead. Kathleen neared the end of the backstretch. She heard quick footsteps and heavy breathing close behind her. She resisted the urge to look over her shoulder, knowing it would only slow her. It was probably Madelyn.

Kathleen's lungs ached and her legs felt numb; she dug in deeper as she neared the curve. This was the last turn and then the homestretch and the finish line. She was almost there.

A blue blur and then a young girl's face flashed in front of her. Someone had dashed into her lane. It was too late to respond. Kathleen heard a scream and felt a sharp pain in her ribs as they collided. Then all was black.

Kathleen opened her eyes and found herself face-down, staring cross-eyed at fat, green blades of grass. The pungent smell of fresh-cut lawn filled her senses.

Where was she? What had happened?

She tried to breathe but couldn't. She rolled onto her back and tried to breathe. Panic seized her as she realized she couldn't. She gasped again. Slowly—her lungs filled with air. She heard heavy breathing; then footsteps rushed past her.

The race! What was she doing on the ground? She'd lost the lead!

"Are you all right? I'm afraid I knocked the wind out of you." A girl in a blue tartan kilt knelt beside her. "I'm sorry I ran out on the track — I didn't see you coming. And now I've taken you both out of the race." The girl untangled her scarf from Kathleen's shoulders and looked anxiously from Kathleen to the other injured race contestant lying on the ground next to her.

Kathleen looked at the girl she had just run into and nodded blankly, but she scarcely comprehended a word the girl had said. Everything was hazy. She put her hand to her throbbing forehead and got to her knees. The field, the anxious faces along the sideline — were spinning. Kathleen steadied herself, ignoring the nausea in her stomach. The only clear vision that stood out was that of the other contestants running on without her.

She had to get up. She had to finish the race.

3

Back in the Race

Therefore, since we are surrounded by so great a cloud of witnesses, let us throw off everything that hinders and the sin that so easily entangles, and let us run with perseverance the race marked out for us.

HEBREWS 12:1

Kathleen jumped to her feet. The ground whirled. She stumbled forward. She couldn't look down. She had to look straight ahead. She must catch up.

Her strength grew with each step. She rounded the last curve; the other runners were in full view. The crowd cheered, but Kathleen barely heard them. She felt like she was in a dream—everything seemed far away, including the other contestants who were now nearing the finish line. Kathleen dug her toes in deeper and pushed harder. She felt as if she were moving in slow motion. The wind blew through her hair, so she knew she was making some speed. Kathleen pushed even harder but... there was nothing she could do. Madelyn crossed the finish line first.

Harsh reality struck Kathleen with all its bleakness. She had lost her first race. Her whole body ached. Her head throbbed, her lungs burned, and her legs stung like fire. But she ran on. As she neared the finish line, the roar of the crowd grew louder. Kathleen had never heard them cheering so loudly. Why were they cheering? Was it for her?

Papa stood behind the finish line, waiting for her with a mixture of concern and tender approval in his eyes.

Kathleen felt like she did when she was a little girl and had fallen and scraped her knee. She had been brave, but now her papa was there, and he'd understand—he'd take all the pain away.

Kathleen crossed the finish line. Her legs gave way, she fell forward, and arms encircled her. The world grew dark and fuzzy. She heard a distant voice say, "She's fainted." It didn't matter. She had finished the race and was safely in her papa's arms.

The next few hours were fuzzy. Kathleen woke up later that evening in her bed with the worst possible headache. It was so severe she didn't care where she was or what was happening—it was just too painful to think.

"What happened? Where am I? My head hurts terribly," Kathleen said.

Kathleen's Shaken Dreams

Mama sat up in her rocking chair, leaned over Kathleen, and placed her hand on her daughter's forehead. "There now, take it easy. You're at home in your own room. See, here's your doll, Hazel, sitting on your nightstand and next to her is your Bible right where it always is." Mama handed Kathleen her doll. "You've slept the afternoon away. See out the window; the sun is already setting."

"But, why have I been sleeping?" Kathleen tried to sit up in bed, but she felt lightheaded and the room began to swirl. "Wh—why am I so dizzy?"

"You had a little head injury . . . during the race today. Don't you remember?" Mama looked searchingly into Kathleen's eyes. "You were in a collision with some other racers. You fell hard. But you got back up and finished the race. You passed out right after you crossed the finish line. Dr. Schmitt examined you. He feared you might have a broken rib as well as a concussion. Thankfully your ribs are all intact, and he thinks your head injury is not too serious. He says it will heal with adequate rest."

"How long will I feel this way?" Kathleen managed to ask.

"That would be a good question for Dr. Schmitt." Mama squeezed her hand. "He promised to check up on you this evening. In fact, I think I hear his car in the driveway."

"Do you have to leave?" Kathleen gripped her mama's hand. With each passing moment, her mind became

clearer—the Highland Games, the race, the girl that ran out in front of her, but after that was all still a shadow. She still felt strange and wasn't ready to be left alone.

"No dear, I'll wait here with you. Papa and Richard can see him in." Mama kissed Kathleen on the forehead.

"Good evening, Kathleen!" Dr. Schmitt called out merrily as he strode through the door. He set his black doctor's bag on her dresser and dug through it. "I'm glad to see my little patient is awake."

"Yes, she just woke up, not even ten minutes ago." Mama stood to greet the doctor.

"A good sleep is to be expected," Dr. Schmitt said, "especially after an injury of this sort, but I'll just check a few things to make sure you're improving like you should." He shined a bright light into Kathleen's eyes. They watered, and she tried her hardest not to blink as he examined her pupils.

"Very good! Very good!" Dr. Schmitt said. He placed the light back in his bag and patted the top of her head. She tried her best to keep from grimacing. The last thing she wanted to do was show any sign of pain. She wanted to be brave.

"Well, you gave us all a scare, but I still think it's only a light concussion. If you show as much determination to heal as you showed in finishing that race, then you'll pull through just fine. Strict bed rest for four days should be all you need."

Kathleen's Shaken Dreams

"Thank you, Dr. Schmitt." Kathleen smiled. "But—do you really mean total bed rest for four whole days?"

He shook his head and frowned a little, but his eyes twinkled. "My, my! You are a spunky one. Whatever made you so determined to finish that race anyway?"

Kathleen was about to explain their morning devotional about running the race of life and being a shining example of the Lord to the very end, but the doctor continued, "I suppose you want to go out and run another race this very minute. It must be that Scottish blood that gives you a unique mixture of stubborn resilience. You might be strong, little lady, but I can't let you overdo it. It will be four full days in bed for you." Dr. Schmitt nodded his head decidedly and looked toward Kathleen's mama to add extra emphasis to his orders.

"I'll make sure she takes it easy." Mama shook Dr. Schmitt's hand. "Thank you so much for stopping by. Can we serve you some dinner before you leave . . . or perhaps a tea cake with strawberry jam?"

Dr. Schmitt laughed as he affectionately patted his large round belly. "Claire, it isn't often I turn down an offer like that. But tonight I'll have to beg you for a rain check. I must hurry over to the Meiers' house, the new family, to check on their little girl—Lucy, I think is her name. Kathleen somehow managed to escape any major injuries from the collision, but poor little Lucy's ankle is quite swollen—might even be broken."

Lucy Meier? She'd fallen too? Kathleen remembered that there were three girls that fell, but she failed

38

to notice who the other racer was. Kathleen replayed in her mind everything that had happened. Lucy must have been the footsteps she'd heard behind her just before the accident. She must've gotten tripped up in the tangle too.

"Poor Lucy! And it was her first race too." Kathleen sighed, but no one heard. Dr. Schmitt and her mama had already left the room.

Later, Kathleen told her papa and mama all about meeting Lucy just before the race. Papa said that Lucy's twisted ankle had prevented her from finishing the race. But due to Kathleen's resolute finish, many people didn't even realize that there was another girl hurt. Unfortunately, Kathleen's parents had been so concerned about Kathleen's well-being that they were among the ones who didn't realize that Lucy had also been injured.

Kathleen found it hard to sleep that night. She tossed and turned, trying in vain to find a comfortable position. Every muscle and joint in her body ached from her collision. Kathleen thought about Lucy a great deal. She wondered why Lucy's brother had such a fascination with Eric Liddell. Where was her brother, for that matter—why couldn't he be there with his sister? Maybe the reason had something to do with Lucy's faraway looks. It was an odd mixture of love, admiration, and deep sadness.

Kathleen sighed. She wondered if she would ever see Lucy again.

Kathleen's Shaken Dreams

"Good morning, my little princess!" Mama said as she placed a tea tray on Kathleen's nightstand. "Are you feeling better this morning, or do you still feel more like a wounded knight than a fair lady?" The smell of steaming waffles laden with pure maple syrup and melted butter filled the room and made Kathleen's stomach growl.

Kathleen stretched out her arms with a hearty yawn, then tenderly rubbed the knot on her head. "I feel fine—though I think I'm a little less chipper than I was yesterday morning." Kathleen smiled sleepily, remembering the bagpipe revelry the morning before.

"So, no flying bedsheets today with noble attempts to save the princess?" They both laughed, and then Kathleen sobered.

"Mama, I can't seem to get Lucy out of my mind. I wonder how she feels this morning. Do you suppose we could ask Dr. Schmitt where she lives?"

"I don't see why not. Maybe I can send a little package of baked goods over to their house—that is, if they aren't just passing through on summer vacation or something."

"Lucy Meier—that's obviously not a Scottish name." Kathleen remembered her bright blue eyes and blonde hair and wondered what her heritage was. "She had a sort of foreign accent—I think it might have been Dutch or something."

"I don't think Meier is Dutch. My mother, your grandmother, is from the Netherlands, you know. But, let's see. Meier sounds German—"

"Yes, you are right! That's what it was, German."

"What's German?" Richard asked, bounding into the room and jumping onto Kathleen's bed. Papa was right behind him.

"I thought that we would have our breakfast and devotionals in bed with you this morning," Papa said, kissing Kathleen on the top of her head.

"That sounds grand. I love breakfast in bed," Kathleen said.

They all chatted and laughed during their "bed picnic," as Richard named it. Then, just before starting the morning devotional, Richard announced that today he would be attending "Kathleen's Cathedral."

"That has a nice ring to it. I really like the fact that you don't have to get all dressed up," Richard said with a sparkle in his eyes. "We should go to Kathleen's Cathedral every Lord's Day." Papa tousled Richard's hair and then he opened the large family Bible.

"Kathleen's Cathedral is an appropriate name, as your brave and determined sister is the heroine and inspiration of my sermon." Papa winked at Kathleen. "I had no idea when I read Hebrews 12:1 yesterday that you, Kathleen, would be such an inspiring illustration of exactly what that passage is talking about. As I said before, the apostle Paul compares a footrace to everyday life—running the race of life. It says to 'run with perseverance the race marked out for us.' In 1 Corinthians 9:24, it says to run as if to win the prize. But life's race isn't a short sprint like the one Kathleen competed in yesterday. It's a long marathon with a series of triumphs, trials, and challenges. Some days you'll be running along the sunlit heights that flourish on the mountains of blessing. The wind is at your back, and your heart is blissfully soaring with the eagles. Then, when you least expect it, there comes a bend in the road, and the path that is set before you may lead to the valley of sorrow. There, the nights grow cold and dark, and the path is full of roots, causing you to stumble. But God is always there — even if the trail is so dark that you can't see Him."

Kathleen nodded in acknowledgement, but her thoughts were far away. She envisioned a highland princess skipping through the fragrant mountain meadows, following a path that suddenly veered toward a dark valley. Tall trees form a canopy above the princess, making it hard to see the gnarly roots and large rocks strewn across the path. The fair princess's heart is gripped with great fear, and she runs blindly, stumbling at every turn. Soon her knees are cut and her silken dress is soiled. She falls on her face, her strength gone. Tears of helplessness spill from her weary eyes. Suddenly she remembers. Her father, the king, has promised a strong knight at her side to guard and protect her. All the little lass has to do is call and He will not only come to comfort and protect her, but He will guide her through the darkness, giving her the courage to continue with grace.

"Kathleen?" Papa's voice broke into Kathleen's thoughts. "Are you listening?"

"Oh, yes, Papa. I guess I was daydreaming a little, but I was thinking about what you were saying."

"All too often, our human nature overcomes us. We try to run the race in our own strength and end up falling flat on our face . . ."

"That's what Kathleen did," Richard interrupted with a laugh. "She fell flat on her face and boy did it look funny, the three girls tumbling head over—" Mother's disapproving glance sobered Richard. "I am sorry you were hurt, Kathleen."

"Thanks, Richard. Oh! And thank you, in advance, for taking over all my household chores while I'm on bed rest." Kathleen patted him reassuringly on the back. She knew how much Richard disliked "girly" household chores.

Richard covered his face with his hands. "Oh, no, I forgot about that."

Everyone laughed.

"Richard, you are right about Kathleen falling, but that doesn't make her a failure," Papa said. "In Isaiah 40, it says that even young men like you grow weary and fall—some never to rise again. But whoever waits on the Lord will have renewed strength—strength not just to run, but to soar victoriously like an eagle. So, in the race of life, it is not stumbling that makes you a loser. It's the failure to call on the Lord's strength, get up, and persevere to the end." Papa looked at Kathleen and Richard.

Kathleen's Shaken Dreams

His eyes shone with admiration. "That may be a lot to understand at your age—you've only just started your race. But remember, I'll always be proud of my children as long as they keep running the race of life with the same determination and perseverance as Kathleen did yesterday."

Kathleen's thoughts wandered back to the highland princess. It was such a beautifully romantic daydream—she had to finish. The knight in shining armor had yet to answer the desperate cry of the princess . . .

"Okay, Richard, time to get off the bed. Kathleen needs to get some rest. You can visit your sister later this afternoon when your favorite radio show comes on," Mama said.

"That's right; there is a special weekend edition of *Amos and Andy* on tonight! O boy! That will be fun. Can we really bring the radio in here?" Richard clapped his hands and jumped off the bed.

"Sure we can." Papa winked at Kathleen. "But it's rather large; I might need your help moving it."

"Yes, sir!" Obviously feeling very important, Richard straightened his shoulders and followed Papa down the hall.

Mama smoothed the pink and yellow patchwork quilt on Kathleen's bed. She turned to leave and then paused at the door. "Get some rest. Remember the doctor's orders."

Kathleen nodded and then let out a long sigh. She could relate to the princess's dark valley. What was she

going to do cooped up in bed for three more days? At least, she would have plenty of time to ponder her daydream. Maybe God wanted to use this time to teach her something special. Kathleen whispered a prayer in her heart.

Dear Lord, You promise in Your Word that You work everything out for good for those who love You. Please help me to be patient in my recovery and help me to see the good that You have already planned for this time.

Kathleen yawned, rubbed her eyes, and cuddled down under the quilt Grandma Maggie had made for her. Before long she drifted into a peaceful sleep.

After her nap, Kathleen propped herself up with an extra pillow her mama had brought and soon lost herself in one of Sir Walter Scott's novels, *The Fair Maid of Perth*. The rest of the day flew by much faster than Kathleen anticipated. Before she knew it, the sun was high in the sky, and her heart was as merry as the birds that chattered above her windowsill.

"Kathleen, do you remember what Wednesday night is?" Papa asked his daughter that afternoon when he came to visit.

"Oh! Goodness gracious. Where is my harmonica? I did forget!" Kathleen sat straight up in bed and placed her hands on her cheeks. "This week is the missionary conference at church—right? And Wednesday evening I'm playing my harmonica during the special offering for support of foreign missions."

45

"That's right. So I guess you'll be busy the next couple of days—even if you are in bed. You definitely have a God-given talent when it comes to music, but you must be diligent to practice if you want to use that gift to glorify Him." Papa smiled as he placed her harmonica and some sheet music on her lap. "If I'm not mistaken, the tune will be 'Rescue the Perishing.' "

"I guess God did have a reason for me to be bedridden! I'll have plenty of time to practice without any distractions," Kathleen said merrily, taking the harmonica and music book from Papa.

4

Mistakes and Rescues

Blessed is he whose transgressions are forgiven,
whose sins are covered.

PSALM 32:1

During Kathleen's confinement, she thought about Lucy Meier quite often and wondered what became of her. Mama had been unable to find any further information about the girl, and Kathleen settled in her mind that she probably would never see Lucy again. But for some reason she couldn't stop thinking about her.

Much to Kathleen's relief, the next few days went by more quickly than she expected. She obeyed the doctor's orders and stayed in bed—at least she stayed seated in one place. Not wanting to miss out on any of the family activities, Kathleen asked if she could make a bed on the living room sofa, where she happily spent the last three days of her confinement.

Kathleen found that if she stayed in the living room, she really didn't miss out on any indoor activities. She could catch the latest news on the *Chicago Morning Show*. After breakfast Kathleen listened to music on the radio while she delved further into the exciting Highland adventures of Sir Walter Scott's novel. Kathleen spent much of the day either practicing the harmonica or reading. Soon, evening shadows cast across the walls, and Kathleen could smell luscious aromas coming from the kitchen. She knew it was almost dinnertime, which meant that another episode of *Amos and Andy* would be on the radio any minute.

By Wednesday evening Kathleen felt sure she was ready for her harmonica solo. Even with all her practice it made her nervous to think of performing in front of so many people. The Wednesday evening service would be the opening to the Missions Conference and there was sure to be a big turnout.

It was with great trepidation that Kathleen situated herself next to Richard in the backseat of their white Chevrolet sedan. As usual, Kathleen had been more than excited to offer to play the special music, but when the time drew near for her to actually stand up in front of the congregation and perform, she became anxious.

The ten minute drive to church seemed to take forever. Even the shiny leather seats of their new sedan did not distract Kathleen from the nervous feeling in her stomach. It was not that she didn't love riding in their new car — it was the nicest one they had ever owned. She

loved the pure white exterior and thought the yellow spoke wheels made their car the smartest-looking vehicle in town.

Kathleen took a deep breath as they pulled into the church parking lot. She nervously smoothed the waistline of her lavender silk dress. The bell tower normally looked beautiful against the setting sun, but today the ornate spire stretched above her and seemed to cast an ominous shadow across her as she walked up the steps to the foyer.

Kathleen took Mama's hand. "Oh! Mama, why do I always agree to do things like this? If only the special music was first—I probably won't be able to focus on a word about foreign missions until the music is over."

"I'm sure you'll survive just fine." Mama glanced at Papa with a curious grin and nodded her head.

They stopped on the patio just outside the door to the foyer.

"Kathleen," said Papa, "your mama and I have a little surprise for you. We were going to wait until after your performance—but I think now would be best. It might help take your mind off being so nervous." He handed Kathleen a small, beautifully wrapped purple package with a gold velvet bow.

"Goodness! What is it?" asked Kathleen, gently taking the pretty package into her hands.

"I guess you could say it's an early birthday present—but really it is a just-because-we-love-you present," Mama said. "We know how much you love surprises."

Kathleen's Shaken Dreams

Mama's eyes twinkled with merriment as Kathleen tried to carefully open the wrapping, but she was so excited that she tore the corners. Inside the wrapping was a little wooden box made of beautiful cherry. Kathleen drew a deep breath as she opened the lid. Inside, cradled in a bed of blue silk, lay an attractive harmonica with intricate, artistic gold engraving on the brass paneling. It read "Trumpet Call" with "Limited Edition, 1929" written beneath.

"Let me see it, Kathleen," Richard said. Kathleen handed him the harmonica. He ran his fingers over the engraving and let out a whistle. "That's mighty fine . . . Papa must have paid a pretty penny for it."

"Wherever did you find this?" Kathleen turned the shiny instrument from side to side, examining it closely. "I've never seen such a beautiful one."

"I saw it in a window display at Taylor Music Store and couldn't pass it up," Mama said.

Kathleen imagined herself standing in front of the church playing her new harmonica, and suddenly her fear melted away. "Thank you, Mama. Thank you, Papa. I will play it tonight."

"Now, Kathleen, this harmonica is much smaller than your old one. The keyholes are positioned differently, so I would not recommend using it for this evening's performance." Mama placed her hand around Kathleen's shoulder as they walked in the foyer together. "You will have to practice quite a bit before you will be as familiar with this new one as you are with your old one."

50

"That would be awfully funny—I mean bad—if you tried it and goofed up," Richard said with a mischievous twinkle in his eye.

Kathleen ignored his comment. She picked the new harmonica out of the case and ran her fingers across the keyholes. Mama was right. They were a little smaller and closer together. She put her mouth to the harmonica and softly blew a note. But surely if she studied the mouthpiece carefully during the sermon, she'd get used to the spacing. After all, Mama had just said all she needed was to become familiar with the new mouthpiece. It couldn't be that much different from her old one. A harmonica was a harmonica.

The organ began to play and Papa led the family from the foyer to a row of seats near the front of the church. Kathleen normally enjoyed hearing about different missionaries in faraway countries, but this evening she was so focused on her new harmonica, she barely heard a word the visiting missionary pastor said. He finished his sermon in what seemed to Kathleen as record time. When it came time to join the others in the choir, Kathleen had only begun to study the keyholes and mentally train herself to make the necessary adjustments.

When the pastor bowed his head to pray, Kathleen knew the time had come. She clutched her new harmonica and quickly made her way out of the pew. She intentionally looked at the ground to avoid her mama's eyes. Kathleen immediately felt a little sting in her conscience and began to get a slight sick feeling in her stomach. Mama had cautioned her not to use the new one.

Should she turn around and get her old one? No, the pastor was almost done praying, and walking back down the row would draw too much attention. Besides, Mama hadn't exactly said that she couldn't use the new harmonica.

Kathleen slid into her seat with the choir and looked out at the congregation. She scanned the crowd. Familiar faces stood out. Papa, Mama, Richard, Dr. Schmitt and his family, Madelyn and Patricia Barnett with their family—the more people she saw, the more butterflies Kathleen felt in her stomach. Near the back of the church she thought she saw a girl with a familiar face, but she couldn't quite see through the crowded pews. She leaned a little to the side to get a better look, but the kind, gray-headed organist, Mr. Pinkerton, started playing the introduction to "Let the Lower Lights Be Burning." The choir, accompanied by the organ, would sing during the tithe and offering. Kathleen then would play her solo, "Rescue the Perishing," during the silent prayer and reflection. The choir stood and Kathleen knew all eyes were on her. She was thankful she wouldn't have to play until the next song. But unfortunately, the full reality of her situation began to sink in. Her part was a solo—she could not afford to make any mistakes.

She shouldn't have made the rash decision to play her new harmonica, but there was nothing she could do

now. The choir finished the first verse and started the refrain:

> Let the lower lights be burning,
> Send a gleam across the waves
> Some poor wrestling fainting seaman
> You may rescue, you may save.

Kathleen's fingers shook as she ran them up and down the keyholes, trying to judge the difference in spacing from her old harmonica. She was glad that she was sitting on the bottom row. The railing hid her hands so that no one could see them moving nervously in her lap.

"Let the Lower Lights Be Burning" came and went, and before she knew it, the choir was ending the hymn. Kathleen felt a stab of panic. She placed the harmonica to her lips. The keyholes felt strange and out of place. She wasn't even sure if she had found the starting note. There was a huge difference between the new and old instrument. Why hadn't she listened to Mama?

The room grew quiet, and Pastor McCarthy announced that there would be a time of silent prayer and reflection. The stillness in the church made Kathleen feel even more nervous. She wanted to run but then had a better thought.

"Lord," she prayed, "You've promised to return. I wouldn't mind if You chose to come and rapture me this very moment. Please . . . I mean, only if it's Your will."

Kathleen's Shaken Dreams

There was a long pause. Mr. Pinkerton, the organist, looked at Kathleen and nodded his head. It was her turn. Kathleen tried to smile as she stood up, took a deep breath, and placed the harmonica back to her mouth.

Kathleen blew into the mouthpiece. Much to her relief, the tone came out clear and on tune. She had hit the right key. The first few notes flowed nicely and Kathleen began to feel fairly confident. Then, without warning—

"Raaaaaaaan."

Kathleen moved the instrument to the left and blew again. It was closer, but she still hit the wrong note and it sounded awfully shaky. Her body trembled. She tried again. It only made things worse. Kathleen decided to just go on to the rest of the song and skip the difficult part. She blew in and out and moved the harmonica to several different keyholes. Quick, high squeaky notes came out, but they failed to follow the tune she had so carefully practiced. She blurted out noisy attempts at a tune, but things went from bad to dreadful. In her nervousness, Kathleen forgot to breathe. All at once, she realized she was blowing her hardest, but nothing was coming out. She stopped and gulped in a deep breath.

Kathleen scanned the crowd. There was a mother correcting her young children, who had been giggling. A couple of rows back sat an older woman trying her hardest to remain steadfast in prayer despite the horri-

ble screeches from the choir loft and the giggling children in front of her. Behind that woman sat Mama and Papa and Richard. Papa's head was bowed. Kathleen couldn't read his expression, but Mama was looking directly into Kathleen's eyes. There was a mixture of tender mercy and disappointment. Mama's look struck Kathleen deep within her heart. She knew she had dishonored her mama by making the wrong decision. As a result, she had disrupted the prayer time, let down her parents, and embarrassed herself beyond belief. She knew her mama was more concerned and hurt by her disobedience than by her hitting the wrong notes.

Kathleen's eyes filled with tears. Even though she had made a bad choice, Kathleen knew she must fulfill her commitment to the best of her ability—even if it meant further embarrassment. She placed the harmonica back to her lips.

She played a few more notes. They were awful.

The organist cleared his throat, pretending to have a slight cough. She looked over at him. He winked at her. His wrinkled face lit with an understanding smile. He played a few notes along with her, picking up where she had left off. Kathleen remained standing and accompanied the best she could. Thankfully, her mistakes were muffled by the deep, strong tones of the pipe organ.

Kathleen had to sit with the choir until the conclusion of the service. It was humiliating waiting there with the whole church before her. She couldn't stop

thinking about the look on her mama's face — Kathleen knew the embarrassment she felt was the result of her disobedience. She had been so excited about playing her beautiful new harmonica that she chose not to listen to her mama's counsel. Kathleen's stomach churned.

Papa's devotional on running the race of life seemed like ages ago. Since then, Kathleen kept finding herself flat on her face in the valley of sorrow rather than soaring on the heights of blessing.

What was it Papa had said about falling on your face? "It's not the falling that disqualifies you, it's the failure to get up and keep running." Did that mean she'd have to admit her mistake, ask forgiveness, and keep on running? Kathleen took a deep breath.

Dear Lord, give me the courage to do this. I really have messed things up. I've dishonored my parents, and as a result, I've distracted the whole congregation from the message in the song. Please forgive me.

Throughout the remainder of the service, the only thing Kathleen could think about was gaining her parents' forgiveness. When the service was over, they were waiting in the foyer. She felt all eyes were on her.

"Mama, I'm so sorry I didn't listen to you." Kathleen blinked to hold back her tears. Mama and Papa put their arms around their daughter and led her toward the doorway.

"I'm afraid you let the anticipation of playing your new instrument rule over your head and your conscience," Mama said. "But of course, I forgive you."

"Papa, I'm sorry I embarrassed you and Mama." Kathleen's heart was full of sorrow as she looked up at her papa.

"You didn't embarrass me. We all make mistakes, lass. Your failure to listen to your mama's counsel is my greatest concern—and I think you've been sufficiently reproved. You needn't worry about it anymore."

The foyer felt crowded and hot and Kathleen could not wait to step outside into the cool night air. They were almost to the door when Mr. Barnett, owner and president of the town's biggest bank, stopped them.

"Mr. McKenzie! How are you this evening?" He strode across the foyer toward them. He didn't even wait for an answer before plunging into talk about business. "I saw your shiny new car outside. I know the construction industry is booming, but I also hear your boss is doing quite well with his investments in the stock market. Isn't this economy amazing? I read that it's never been this good in the history of our country."

Kathleen stood, afraid to move. She hoped that if she were still enough he wouldn't notice her, but her efforts were in vain.

"It was good talking with you, Mr. McKenzie," Mr. Barnett said. "Oh! And I almost forgot. Thank you for your little performance this evening, Miss Kathleen. It was very—that was very courageous of you to get up in front of all those people."

"You're welcome, sir." Kathleen blushed crimson.

Kathleen's Shaken Dreams

"We'll see you Sunday," Papa said as he shook Mr. Barnett's hand.

Once they were finally outside, Richard came up beside her. "It wasn't all that bad—really. I mean, it didn't sound too great—the little boy in front of me covered his ears and made all sorts of faces—but I never had so much fun." The more Richard talked, the more humiliated Kathleen felt. Then, much to Kathleen's surprise, Mama let out a little giggle; Papa chuckled, and before long the whole family had burst into laughter. Even Kathleen found the humor in the situation and laughed until tears streamed down her cheeks.

She shrugged. "Well, at least I was entertaining. I guess we'll still be laughing about this years from now—only then I'm sure I'll find it less humiliating than I do now."

"Kathleen McKenzie? Is that you?" A girl approached her on crutches. "I was hoping I'd catch you before you took off. I never did get to see you after the race, and I didn't want to miss you again."

Kathleen recognized the familiar face she had seen at the back of the church just before her performance.

"Lucy? Lucy Meier?" The headlights from someone's car turned on, and Kathleen could see her face clearly. Poor Lucy looked a little wobbly on her crutches, but she still had the same bright smile that lit up her whole face.

5

A Birthday Surprise

*Your love, O Lord, reaches to the heavens,
your faithfulness to the skies.*
PSALM 36:5

That night in the parking lot of the church, Kathleen learned Lucy had just moved to Fort Wayne, and best of all, she lived in the McKenzies' neighborhood. They exchanged phone numbers, and as soon as Lucy's ankle healed, the girls were able to see each other often. The Meiers lived a little over a mile away, and they would roller-skate, meeting each other halfway.

Lucy was the youngest of five sisters. Kathleen knew she also had an older brother who she was quite fond of, but Kathleen never saw him and Lucy rarely mentioned him. All of Lucy's sisters lived at home except for the oldest, who was married. Lucy's sisters dressed similarly and looked an awful lot alike with their long eyelashes, blue eyes, and bright, rosy lips.

59

They even curled the ends of their blonde hair and combed it the same way too.

"They are all so kind, but no matter how hard I try, I can never remember who's who," Kathleen said one night while talking to her mother about Lucy's family. "The oldest is Dottie; she's married. Then Deanna is the nurse. Next comes Helen, who is getting her teaching degree—or is Helen the nurse and Deanna getting the teaching degree? Rose, I believe, is a senior in high school—no, Rose is in college and Helen is the senior. Oh dear, I'm not so sure I'll ever get them straight."

Over the next month, hardly a day went by that Kathleen and Lucy did not see each other. Kathleen had lots of friends at church and school, but Lucy was unlike any girl she'd ever met—so transparent that it seemed she could not hide a thing she was thinking, and yet so kind that nothing unpleasant or negative ever seemed to slip out from her lips. There was nothing pretentious about Lucy, and although the Meiers lived in the biggest house in the neighborhood, she was humble, sincere, and sweet.

As summer drew to a close, Kathleen and Lucy spent many afternoons in Kirk's Woods playing in Kathleen's favorite hideout down by the river. The shady woods were at the edge of their neighborhood and were only a half mile from the McKenzies' home. Together they built a makeshift playhouse out of a few pieces of driftwood they had found on the banks of the river. It didn't look like much, but with the help of their

imaginations, it served many purposes. On some days it was a grand castle. The girls, along with Kathleen's cloth doll Hazel and Lucy's beautiful porcelain doll Belle, would pretend they were at a formal high tea in a grand hotel parlor. On other days, their hideout was a frontier fort and they were on an expedition far out West with mountain men, James Bridger and Kit Carson, seeking to discover new lands. It was there, in her makeshift playhouse, that Kathleen told Lucy all about her friends and teachers at Hogeland School.

"You'll like the teachers. Miss Brooklin, our language teacher, makes the least interesting subjects exciting. I know, I had her last year," Kathleen said while sweeping the dirt floor in preparation for another grand tea party. "And I hear Miss Blake is the kindest woman and has a way of teaching history that makes you feel like you have gone back in time and are actually living in the era that you're studying." Kathleen stopped and leaned against the broom handle to catch her breath. "I love history, just like my papa. He says that someday he hopes to take the family on vacation to Washington, D.C., so we can see all the historic sights. Anyway, I can't wait to study history with Miss Blake."

"What about the students in our class? What are they like?" Lucy asked, as she spread on the ground a light green piece of cloth covered with a pattern of white lilies. It was a scrap of material left over from a summer dress Kathleen's mother had sewn for her. It made the perfect tablecloth for their tea.

Kathleen's Shaken Dreams

"Oh! Our classmates are great. I'm sure you will get along just fine with all of them — all except for Jake and Dan. They are the school bullies. Jake likes to tell scary stories about an old hermit he claims lives in these woods — "

"Really? In these woods?" Lucy looked around with concern written on her face.

"But I'm sure they're not true. He thinks that just because he and Dan are a head taller than the rest of us that they can push everyone around and play mean pranks. And then there is Patricia Barnett. You may remember her older sister, Madelyn, from the race at the Highland Games. They come to our church from time to time. They are nice enough, I guess, but they think that they own the whole school just because their father owns the bank up the street. But don't worry about them — the rest of the class is fantastic, especially Grace, Carrie, and Freddie. I can't wait for you to meet them. I'm sure they will love you too."

"I can't wait for school to begin. Won't it be fun to study our homework together? We can even come here to study." Lucy clapped her hands together in excitement. "And the teachers and classmates sound so nice."

Kathleen was delighted to find that Lucy shared her love for school. They could spend hours making plans for the upcoming fall semester. When school finally did come, Kathleen and Lucy were glad to find that they were not only in the same seventh grade class, but also seated right next to each other. When Kathleen rushed

home to tell her parents the good news, Mama just smiled at Papa with a knowing look and said, "I had a feeling that might happen."

"You requested that for me, didn't you?" Kathleen threw her arms around her mama's neck. Mama didn't say a thing, but Kathleen knew better. Papa and Mama made it their business to befriend their children's teachers and were involved as much as possible with each aspect of their education.

Kathleen loved the fall season for two reasons. Not only did school start, but there was another thing that Kathleen always looked forward to, October 5—her birthday.

Finally, the first week in October came, and it was the night before the big day. Kathleen lay wide awake in her bed. Twelve sounded so much older than eleven. Lucy's older sister Helen had said that twelve-year-olds had a much more mature outlook on life. Kathleen wondered if she would look older. She'd still have freckles— Mama said they would fade eventually, but she thought they were only growing darker.

Kathleen sighed. Her thoughts turned to her birthday present. For the last couple of weeks, Papa and Richard had been busily working on Kathleen's birthday surprise in the garage, and she was not allowed to enter. They had been so secretive about the project that Kathleen was about to burst with curiosity. The last several days, though, Mama had given her so much housework that she hardly had time to think about the birthday project. Each day Kathleen had worked hard hoping to finish in time to play with Lucy down by their fort, but it seemed her lists of chores never ended. Wash the windows, clean the bathrooms, straighten her room, and vacuum. Kathleen didn't mind the last chore. Papa had purchased one of the new electric Hoover vacuum cleaners for Mama, and Kathleen loved to run it over the carpet and watch as it sucked up all the dust. It seemed miraculous to her, and it was twice as fast as the old push broom. Kathleen was amazed as she thought of how much housework Mama and she had accomplished in so short an amount of time.

To Kathleen, it was almost like Mama had her seasons mixed up. The workload seemed more like spring cleaning. But it had helped the time go by quickly — after all, her birthday was tomorrow and she would find out what the great surprise was. Kathleen finally drifted off to sleep.

After breakfast Mama presented her with a large box secured tightly with a bright red bow attached. The card read:

Happy Birthday!
To my dear daughter, Kathleen Margaret McKenzie
From your ever-loving Mama

Kathleen looked up at her papa in surprise. "Papa, why isn't your name on my present?"

Papa's eyes twinkled, and he tried to hide his smile. "It's really from both of us, but this gift was your

mama's idea, and since it goes nicely with the present Richard and I have been working on—"

"You mean there's more than one gift?" Kathleen exclaimed. Papa had said that God had blessed him financially this last year, but Kathleen was amazed that they had that much money to spend. "I can't believe it. Thank you so much."

"Thank you?" Richard shifted in his chair impatiently. "You haven't even opened it yet. Hurry, I can hardly wait to bring you down to the river to show you our—" Richard quickly put his hand over his mouth. "Oops! I mean—"

"Yes," said Mama, "that's right, Kathleen. We thought you could invite Lucy over for lunch and we'd all have a picnic down by the river."

Kathleen's mind raced. So that was why Mama had kept her so busy the past few days. She wanted to keep her away from the river. But why?

The last of the wrapping came off and Kathleen breathlessly peered into the box. Inside was the most beautifully dressed doll. She had a delightful porcelain face and lively green eyes. Kathleen had seen her a hundred times in the Wolf and Dessauer's Department Store window. She was the latest doll on the market, and they advertised her to be so well made that her porcelain face was unbreakable.

"Mama! How did you know? I dreamed of playing with her, but never imagined I would actually own her. I thought she was too much."

Kathleen's Shaken Dreams

"Your mama and I thought that given your—well, shall we say, spunky nature—we would give you a doll that could tackle life's exciting adventures right along with you."

"Oh, goodness! She's too beautiful to face life in the great outdoors with me." Kathleen studied the doll's delicate rosy lips and cheeks, and long curly lashes, and stroked her shiny auburn locks. "Breakable or not—I will take especially good care of her."

The new doll made Kathleen even more curious about Papa's surprise. Maybe it was a dollhouse. Or a doll chair so Kathleen could display her lovely doll on her dresser.

"What a wonderful birthday gift," Lucy said, carefully touching the beautiful lace on the doll's collar. "She is the most beautiful doll I've ever seen." The girls had brought the porcelain doll upstairs to Kathleen's bedroom. "What are you going to name her?" asked Lucy.

The door flew open. It was Richard. "Mama says it's time."

"We'll be right there. Lucy and I were just discussing our favorite names."

"Your favorite names? What for? What's wrong with Lucy and Kathleen?"

"No, no. We aren't changing *our* own names. We're naming Kathleen's doll." Lucy laughed.

"Well, I wish you'd be quick about it. It's time for your picnic, Kathleen, and boy, am I hungry!" Richard patted his stomach.

"Okay, what do you think of the name Marguerite?" asked Lucy.

"Margue—what?" Richard wrinkled his nose.

"Marguerite. It is a French name that means 'daisy,'" said Lucy. "Marguerite is the name of the fair lady in Baroness Emma Orczy's book, *The Scarlet Pimpernel*. You must read it! That's one of my brother's favorites."

"I'd rather not," Richard said under his breath. "I don't care whose brother likes it—it sounds girly."

"I've heard it is a wonderful book and I like the sound of that name. Marguerite it shall be!" Kathleen nodded her head decisively.

Richard flopped onto the bed. "Why not just call her Daisy? I've never heard of that other fancy name. It sounds funny if you ask me."

"Daisy is too common," said Kathleen, running her fingers softly over the doll's fine hair. "Marguerite sounds like royalty from a faraway land—probably from France. But maybe her father was from England or even from Scotland, so she grew up speaking English . . ." Kathleen's voice trailed off as she envisioned a castle where her doll princess might have lived.

"Ladies, your picnic awaits you!" Mama called from the kitchen.

Richard jumped to his feet and they all raced downstairs to where Papa and Mama waited.

67

Kathleen's Shaken Dreams

"Don't you think Kathleen should be blindfolded first?" asked Richard.

Kathleen's heart leapt as Papa placed a red scarf over her eyes. What a fun mystery gift this had been and now she could finally find out what it was.

Despite the blindfold, it didn't take long for the small party to make their way out the front door and through the woods toward the banks of St. Mary's River. Kathleen placed her hand on Papa's strong arm and let him lead her. Richard eagerly called out every stump and rock that Kathleen might trip over.

Lucy chatted merrily with Mrs. McKenzie about the large picnic basket she was helping her carry. "I can't wait to see what sort of goodies are inside, Mrs. McKenzie! You are one of my favorite cooks. I'm so excited we're eating a picnic lunch. My mama says it's all in my head, but I'm convinced food tastes better when you eat it outside."

The anticipation was so great that it was all Kathleen could do to keep from running blindly down the path. Finally Kathleen could feel the dirt path sloping down, and she knew they were nearing the river. Soon they would be shaded beneath the lush foliage of the maple and elm trees that grew near the bank.

The Best Birthday Gift Ever

*Every good and perfect gift is from above, coming down from the
Father of the heavenly lights, who does not change like shifting
shadows.*

JAMES 1:17

"Here's the chestnut tree!" shouted Richard.

Lucy gasped. "Mr. McKenzie, you mean to tell me that you built—that's incredible! How did you get it up so high?"

"High?" Kathleen asked excitedly. "What's high? Can I take off my blindfold?"

Just then the blindfold fell from her eyes and Kathleen squinted to adjust to the afternoon sun.

"Look, Kathleen." Richard pointed upward into the chestnut tree. "Papa and I built it all by ourselves!"

Kathleen stared in disbelief. There, in the tree above her old makeshift fort, perched a large rectangular tree house complete with window boxes, a swing, a rope ladder, and an escape hatch with a knotted rope hanging down to the ground. Kathleen opened her mouth to speak, but was so amazed she couldn't find the words to express what she felt.

"Richard and I decided not to paint your playhouse," Papa said. "We thought you and Lucy might want to choose all the colors and do the interior decorating." Papa grinned and put his arm around Mama. "If you're anything like your mama, you'll be quite the interior decorator."

Kathleen stammered, "Thank you! I—I can't believe you made it . . . and it's for me! Thank you so—"

"Come on, let's go look inside." Richard pulled on her arm. He appeared just as excited as, if not more than, his sister.

Kathleen started toward the rope ladder and then turned back to Papa and Mama and gave them a big hug and thanked them again.

Mama laughed. "I didn't help build it, but your little brother did, and I don't think he can wait another minute to show you inside."

While Papa and Mama spread the picnic blanket and set out the food, Richard gave Kathleen and Lucy the grand tour of the one-room tree house. On the opposite wall from the doorway, there was a built-in table and chairs for two. Just above the table was a window with wooden shutters.

Richard pointed at the larger window to the right of the table. "This was my idea. It looks like a big window, but really it's the escape route. After Jake told me about

how that scary old hermit kidnapped that helpless little girl, I decided it was a must."

"Scary old hermit?" Lucy raised her eyebrows in question. "I thought that was just a story Jake made up to frighten people."

Kathleen scowled at Richard.

"Well, maybe it is," said Richard. "But you never know what's in the forest. So, if the dreaded enemy comes up the ladder, all you have to do is slip out this window and slide down this rope." Richard stuck his foot out the window to demonstrate, but just before sliding down, he poked his head back in. "Of course, you'll never need to worry about the enemy coming up either the rope ladder or this one because you can pull it up—just like a castle drawbridge."

Kathleen smiled. Richard knew her dreamy nature all too well.

The picnic lunch that followed was perfect in every way. Mama had prepared all of Kathleen's favorite foods: an orange sherbet congealed fruit salad, chicken potpie, and cream puffs for dessert. The food was delicious, but Kathleen agreed with Lucy, eating outdoors made it twice as good. She breathed deeply and took in the beauty surrounding her. The sun was high in the sky, but the large red maples lining the river shaded their picnic area. The unseasonably warm temperature combined with the gentle fall breeze made it an idyllic day for a picnic. Occasionally a swift gust of wind made the colorful autumn leaves shimmer as they glided down and painted the river-banks in their rich colors.

After lunch, Richard, Lucy, and Kathleen searched the ground for the largest, fastest-looking maple leaves for mini-boat races. They launched their little vessels, consisting of tiny twig masts and small chestnut leaf sails, into the steady current and ran alongside and cheered as the ships bobbed up and down in the crystal waters. The first vessel to reach the bend was declared the winner. Then they ran back to the starting line to start over again with a newer, faster model.

Papa joined them after a while, and before long Mama did too. They all laughed and cheered until their sides ached. All too soon, the sun was sinking in the western sky, and it was time to go home.

Mama, Papa, and Richard set out walking, but the girls lingered behind. Kathleen took one more longing look at her tree house. It seemed so inviting, nestled high in the thick branches of the tree. She sighed, hating the thought of leaving. Then, all of a sudden, Kathleen had a splendid idea.

"Lucy! Why don't you and I camp out in my tree house tonight?"

"Oh! Could we? That would be such an adventure! Do you think it would be okay with your parents for just the two of us to be out alone?"

"Sure . . . Then we could plan all the home improvements it needs — you know, things like paint colors, curtains, rag rugs, bulbs for the flowerboxes — things that

will make it homier." She paused. In her excitement she had barely heard Lucy's question about whether or not they would be allowed to camp out. She pondered the question for a brief moment and rushed on. "Surely it will be okay. The tree house is not even a quarter mile from the house." Kathleen rushed to catch up with her parents and asked their permission.

"Are you girls all situated up there?" Papa called from the bottom of the drawbridge rope.

Kathleen looked down from the tree house. "Yes, Papa. It's so cozy up here! I'm sure we'll sleep as snug as bugs in a rug."

"Good night then, girls—the house is not far if you need anything. And don't forget, your lantern must be off in thirty minutes."

"We won't forget. Good night," the girls called in unison.

Kathleen watched her papa slowly disappear through the woods. His lantern swung back and forth making the shadows from the nearby trees double in size. Suddenly, Kathleen felt very small compared to the dark woods that surrounded them.

"Let's see, what home improvements should we discuss first?" Lucy held her lantern up and examined the four walls of the tree house. The light shining on her face made Lucy's usual bright smile even more soothing, and Kathleen's unsettled feeling melted away.

73

Kathleen's Shaken Dreams

"I think we should paint the outside yellow, then wallpaper the interior with the blue and white daisy pattern that was left over from my mama's parlor." Kathleen ran her fingers over the rough wooden walls. "Then maybe I can use my allowance to buy material to make matching curtains. We would have to get at least five yards, maybe even more, if we want nice ruffled curtains. I learned how to sew ruffles in my home economics class last year at school." Kathleen's excitement rose as she spoke. "They require lots of material, and Mama thinks I should learn to sew proficiently by hand before I am allowed to use her new Singer electric sewing machine, so it may take a long time. But I think it will be worth it. I love full curtains."

Papa had given them his watch before he left, and all too soon their thirty minute curfew was up.

The night air rapidly grew colder, and they were grateful Mama had insisted on sending a large pile of warm quilts for them to nestle between. Kathleen blew out the lantern and for a moment, all was pitch black.

"My, it *is* dark in here, isn't it?" Lucy whispered.

"It sure is. Did you notice if the moon was out tonight?"

"I didn't really notice, but now that my eyes are adjusting, it does look like a little bit of moonlight is shining through the windows," Lucy answered.

Kathleen listened. The chorus of crickets blended with the soft breeze that rustled in the trees. Occasionally, Kathleen would hear the far-off song of a night lark calling to its mate. All seemed so peaceful that Kathleen laughed at herself for being so fearful.

Kathleen realized that Lucy had not said a word since she'd blown out the red lantern. "Are you still awake?" Kathleen whispered.

"Yes." Lucy's reply was soft—almost wistful, reminding Kathleen of the faraway look Lucy had gotten in her eyes the day they met.

"You're awfully quiet. What are you thinking about?"

"My brother, Peter. He and I used to sleep out in my grandparents' hayloft on their farm."

In all these weeks, Lucy had rarely brought up her brother's name. In fact, at times, Kathleen almost forgot she even had a brother. It occurred to Kathleen that he must have died. Poor Lucy had been bearing this burden alone, and Kathleen hadn't even realized it.

"I'm—I'm sorry about your brother. How long has he been gone?"

"The last time I saw him was just before we moved, but it seems like years ago," Lucy said. Oddly enough her voice didn't seem to hold as much sorrow as Kathleen would have expected.

"I know I haven't talked a lot about him—and that's not because I don't care much for him. I just miss him so much that if I let myself think about him too much, it makes me sad. Mama says that when I'm looking forward to something, the best way to make the time go by quickly is not to think about it."

"I can only imagine how hard it must be." Kathleen gently squeezed Lucy's hand.

"Oh, believe me, not thinking about him is harder on me than most people! Especially when I know that I'll get to be with him sometime around Thanksgiving."

"You'll be with him?" Kathleen leaned up on one elbow, trying to see her friend in the dark. "That's a terrible thing to say—what would I do without you? I understand you miss your brother and all, but I don't think it's right to wish to be with him that much!" Kathleen was horrified. What could she say to change Lucy's mind?

She searched her memory for a verse from the Bible.

Dear Lord, please help me to convince Lucy not to desire such an awfully morbid thing as death, just to be with her brother.

"What do you think is so wrong with wanting to see him?" Lucy sounded surprised and a little defensive.

"Well—it's not the wanting to see him part—it's just that—well, I can't think of the right verse, but I don't think that God intended that a person take her own life just to see a loved one who is in Heaven."

"Take my own life? What? See him in Heaven?" Lucy giggled.

"What's so funny?" Kathleen asked, quite bewildered.

"You think . . . you think my brother is dead?"

"Isn't that what you said?" Kathleen's puzzlement grew by the moment.

"I said that I missed him — but I never said he was dead. Whatever gave you that idea? My grandpa's health began to fail right before we moved to Fort Wayne, and Peter stayed in Michigan with them to help run the farm. My family and I are going to visit them over Thanksgiving weekend."

"Oh! Now I see what you mean." Kathleen sighed in relief and then started to laugh right along with Lucy.

"I can't believe you thought he was dead — I'll have to tell Peter about that. I can't wait to tell him about you, period. He'll be so glad that I've found such a good friend. And not just any friend, but a fast Scottish girl who runs in the Highland — "

Something rustled the branches outside the tree house, and then there was a loud thud. Kathleen couldn't tell if it was on the little porch outside the doorway or right above it.

"What was that?" Kathleen whispered.

Lucy lay frozen next to her — apparently too frightened to speak.

"It's probably a raccoon," said Kathleen, trying to reassure Lucy. But it sounded bigger than that. Kathleen realized that she'd forgotten to pull up the rope ladder. Her heart beat a little faster as she remembered the stories Jake Thomson, the neighborhood bully, had told her. She had never believed him, thinking he was just trying to scare her, but now she recalled every last word. It was almost like Jake was right there whispering it in her ear:

Kathleen's Shaken Dreams

There's an old hermit who lives in a cabin hidden deep within Kirk's Woods. He hates people—especially children who invade "his territory." They call him Bootleggin' Bob because of the illegal moonshine liquor he makes. One night, years ago, a girl disappeared in these woods never to be seen again. The authorities immediately tried to track Bootleggin' Bob but never found his hideout—or any trace of the girl.

Kathleen's heart froze and she fixed her eyes on the window, trying her hardest to discern any possible form in the darkness. But all was still. Nothing moved.

In the distance, Kathleen thought she heard a high-pitched cry. Then everything was silent—all but the faint breeze stirring the fall leaves. Even the crickets seemed too frightened to make any noise.

Was that the wind—or something else? Was she hearing things? The cry came again. Closer this time.

The Mysterious Cry

For God has not given us a spirit of fear, but of power and of love and of a sound mind.

2 TIMOTHY 1:7 (NKJV)

With each new noise Kathleen imagined what kind of person or predator it might be. How could she and Lucy escape? Kathleen tried to be strong, but with each passing second fear crept into her heart until her resolve to be brave weakened.

What could they do?

She dared not move. Yelling wouldn't help—no one could hear them. Besides, that would only alert the culprit to their exact location. Kathleen felt like crying, but she knew that wouldn't help either. Kathleen remembered what her papa had said about being in the valley of sorrow—that sometimes it may be so dark that you can't see Him, but God would always be right there with you. Papa had said all she had to do was cry out for help . . . yes, that was right. Her Bible memory verse in

Sunday school last week said that God would never leave her or forsake her! And what was that verse Mama always said when she was little and feared that there was a robber under her bed or someone hiding in her closet? Something about not having fear in your heart? That's what it was. "God does not give us a spirit of fear, but of love, power and a sound mind." A sound mind, that's what she needed. *Lord*, she prayed to herself, *please help me think clearly*.

There was a scraping sound on the roof, followed by a loud, "Whoooo! Whoooo!"

Both Lucy and Kathleen jumped straight toward each other in alarm — meeting in the middle and knocking heads. "Ouch," they both cried, rubbing the spot where it hurt. Then reality sank in.

"It's just an old owl," Kathleen said, sounding like she had not been in the least bit scared.

"A big, old owl," Lucy said with a strained, shaky laugh. The owl hooted again, and they heard the swish of his wings in the wind as he flew away. They were so relieved that Kathleen forgot about the far-off cries that she had heard just moments before. But before she could say another word, the cry came again, and this time it was closer.

"Did you hear that?" Lucy whimpered. "I don't think it is a good idea for us to be sleeping in the woods all — "

The pitiful cry came again.

"It sounds like a person calling for help, like they're in desperate trouble or — "

"It sounds like a little girl." Lucy grabbed Kathleen's hand.

"She must be in terrible trouble," Kathleen whispered.

The cry came again, and this time Kathleen was sure she heard: "Helllllppp!" Lucy's fingernails cut into Kathleen's skin.

"Lucy, we've got to do something!" Kathleen jumped to her feet.

"Do something? Don't you think it's too dangerous?"

"We can't just sit here and listen to a person crying out for help." Kathleen thought for a moment.

"I'm scared, Kathleen."

"Shhh!" Kathleen tried to sound more confident than she felt. "I am too, but you can't let yourself be — or at least try not to let yourself dwell on it. Someone's life could be at risk. Besides, God doesn't give us a spirit of fear — only the devil and our own imaginations do that." Kathleen surprised herself with her growing confidence. Quoting that verse really did help.

"But what can we do?" Lucy whispered hoarsely.

"Here's what we have to do. First, we need to fetch Papa — he'll know what to do."

"Fetch him in — in the dark? Are you sure?"

"I think I can make it to the house without a lantern." Kathleen felt around in the dark for her shoes. She could hear Lucy doing the same. She crawled over to the door and felt for the rope ladder. She grabbed it and handed it to her friend.

Kathleen's Shaken Dreams

"Lucy, can you see to climb down?"

"I can see. But will you go in front of me?" Lucy's voice trembled.

"Okay, I'll go first." Kathleen climbed down the ladder and held it for Lucy. When Lucy was safely on the ground, Kathleen took her icy hand. "Follow me. It'll be okay."

Kathleen slowly led the way through the dark woods. The dried leaves crunched underfoot making it difficult to walk quietly. Kathleen wondered how in the world the Indians used to sneak through the woods without making a sound.

The cry came again; it was closer. They broke into a run.

They came to a small meadow near the edge of the woods and stopped. Normally it was an inviting place—full of flowers in the spring and summer and colchicum in the fall. Now the sliver of moon cast shadows that made it look threatening.

"Do you think we should run through it or go around?" Kathleen's voice was so faint that Lucy had to lean toward her to hear it.

"It's not a big meadow. Let's just sneak through," whispered Lucy.

"Okay, follow me." Kathleen got down on her hands and knees and crawled through the knee-high grass.

They were halfway across when the inhuman cry came from the edge of the meadow directly to the side of them. Lucy whimpered and Kathleen gasped.

"Let's get out of here." Kathleen grabbed Lucy's hand and sprinted toward her house.

The girls arrived on the McKenzies' porch, out of breath and shivering with fear. Kathleen pounded on the front door. Finally, the light turned on. It felt like an eternity before Papa, in a half-awake stupor, opened the door. The girls rushed past him, almost knocking him off balance. Papa scratched his head and raised one eyebrow. He looked confused.

"Shut the door! Quick!" Kathleen shouted.

Papa slowly shut the door with one hand and motioned for her to be quiet with the other. "Shhhh! You will wake the whole house. Now, what's the matter? Has something scared you? Are you alright?" he whispered.

Kathleen's and Lucy's words tumbled over each other as they told their story.

Papa seemed quite concerned, but when they described the cry, he relaxed and shook his head. "Well, girls, it sounds like you've behaved quite gallantly. I think I might know where this mysterious noise is coming from. If I am right, all will be well in no time." He disappeared into his bedroom. When he returned, he was still wearing his nightshirt, but he had added his work pants and boots. He held his hat in one hand and a revolver in the other.

"Wh—what are you going to do?" Kathleen asked.

"I'm going to clear Kirk's Woods of any possible enemies that would endanger my daughter and her young friend. Stay here until I return." Papa tipped his

hat in a matter-of-fact way and stepped out the door, vanishing into the darkness beyond.

At that moment, Kathleen knew that her papa was the greatest and bravest man she had ever met.

Lucy and Kathleen retreated to the sitting room. They sat close to each other on the sofa, anxiously awaiting Papa's return. Kathleen watched the clock over the fireplace mantel. Eleven fifty-one and ten seconds, eleven fifty-one and eleven seconds. The second hand ticked slowly by.

"What do you suppose is taking so long?" Lucy asked after several minutes had passed.

"I don't know, but I sure wish Papa had not told me to wait here—what if he's in trouble?"

"Maybe we should wake your mama," Lucy suggested.

The clock on the mantel struck midnight and there was a noise at the front door.

Kathleen jumped to her feet and raced to open it. "Papa, is that you?"

Papa walked in confidently. "Twelve o'clock and all is well."

"Did you find anything? Is everything okay?" Lucy asked, her eyes wide with questions.

"Yes, Kirk's Woods are once again free of any dangers." Papa chuckled as he took off his hat.

"Who was it? What did you do?" Kathleen couldn't believe how relaxed her papa was and couldn't figure out what he kept chuckling about.

"I went down to the edge of the clearing where you last heard the cry and sat for some time. All was silent. Not even the screech of an owl or bark from a neighborhood dog. The best I could figure was that you two startled the mysterious being just as much as it startled you. So I moved deeper into the woods, closer to the river. Then, I heard it."

"I knew it wasn't just our imaginations! Did you hear the call for help?" Kathleen asked.

"Yes and no." Papa shook his head and grinned. "You see, in the neighborhood across the river lives an older couple who raise peacocks. Normally, they are too far away to be heard. But evidently one of them escaped and found its way across the bridge and into Kirk's Woods. Peacocks are funny animals. They strut around prouder than any other bird most of the time. But at night in the woods, a peacock is an easy meal for a large owl or big raccoon. They let out a terrifying cry when they sense danger of any kind."

"You mean what we heard was only a measly little peacock?" Kathleen plopped herself onto the couch. "I'm sure we heard someone crying for help. What a disappointment."

"Yes, their cry does sound a little like a muffled, drawn-out 'help' and this was one scared peacock!"

"Goodness gracious! All that for nothing — I'm sorry we woke you up, Papa." Kathleen was baffled and a little embarrassed.

Kathleen's Shaken Dreams

"Don't worry. That's what papas are for—to make sure that their little girls sleep safe and sound at night with sweet dreams. Now, you two need to get some sleep." Papa kissed Kathleen on the forehead and bid them both "good night."

Never before had Kathleen been so grateful to snuggle beneath the covers of her own bed.

"I am glad to know it was just a peacock and not someone in danger." Lucy yawned. She fluffed her pillow and settled in on the other side of the bed.

"Yes, I am too," Kathleen whispered back. "I'm thankful God protected us, even if things weren't as serious as they appeared."

Soon the adventure of the evening seemed far away, and Kathleen drifted peacefully off to sleep.

Triumph and Tragedy

Trust in the LORD with all your heart and lean not on your own understanding; in all your ways acknowledge him, and he will make your paths straight.

PROVERBS 3:5–6

Over the next week, Kathleen and Lucy did their homework as efficiently as possible and spent the rest of their afternoons adding homey touches to the four bare walls of the tree house. As promised, Richard painted the exterior a sunny daffodil yellow. Mama took Kathleen to the fabric store to pick out material for curtains. There were so many bolts of cloth with bright cheery prints that it made it a hard choice. They finally decided on a bolt of cream-colored material with delicate yellow butterflies on it.

"Do you think this looks good with the yellow paint on the exterior?" Kathleen held the fabric up to the trim around the tree house window for Lucy to see.

Kathleen's Shaken Dreams

"I think it's a perfect blend!" said Lucy. "Let's start making them right now."

Kathleen laughed at her enthusiasm and then pointed out the reality. "We'll need to get scissors, some thread, and a needle first. And—we must finish our homework. The spelling bee's next Tuesday and I need to practice. The competition is even tougher than last year, and I would so like to win this time. Last year I came in third behind Freddie Schmitt and Patricia Barnett. Losing to Freddie is understandable; he works hard and Papa says he's as sharp as a tack, but losing to Patricia—now that's a whole different story. She's so keen on herself that she paraded around the whole campus like she was a queen just because she placed second. I know I shouldn't care how she responded—it's not my responsibility. But regardless of that, I determined last year that I would study twice as hard before the next competition." Kathleen sighed and grew silent.

She was doing it again, getting all uptight about a competition.

Dear Lord, please help me to study hard so I can win—I want to do my best with the gifts You've given me, but no matter what happens, whether I win or lose, please help me to be humble, Lord. Help me to shine, not burn.

Spelling was definitely not one of Lucy's strengths. She had already told Kathleen that although she would be participating, she didn't really care about winning.

"I know," said Lucy. "I can drill you on the spelling words while you sew, and then you can drill me and I'll sew! That way we can do both."

"It's a deal. Let's run to the house and get my sewing basket." Kathleen never turned down an opportunity to accomplish two things at once.

The next few days, Kathleen spent most of her time practicing for the spelling bee. Lucy drilled her in the afternoons at the tree house.

"Expedient," Lucy called out as she set the table for a tea party with their dolls.

"E-x-p-e-d-i-e-n-t," Kathleen spelled.

"Correct," Lucy said.

"That was an easy one. I hope I get one like that the day of the spelling bee."

"You only have ten more." Lucy looked up from the list. "Then can we have our tea party? Mama sent some German apple strudel for us to snack on. It's my favorite."

Each evening, Kathleen spent more time practicing. Mama called out words, as Kathleen helped set the table or peeled potatoes for supper. Papa conducted a practice spelling bee for both Richard and Kathleen in the living room each night before bed. By Thursday night, Kathleen felt ready for the next day's competition.

The day of the spelling bee, it appeared that Kathleen's diligent practice was paying off. Everyone had misspelled

a word and had to sit down except for Kathleen and Freddie Schmitt. Even though the school bell had rung, ending the school day, the class remained in their seats, anxiously waiting to see who would be the winner.

"Kathleen and Freddie, are you ready to continue?" Miss Brooklin asked from the front of the room.

They both nodded in reply. Kathleen caught Lucy's eye and mouthed, "Pray for me." Kathleen glanced at Freddie. He had a funny twinkle in his eyes. It reminded her of the look he had at the Highland Games when she had mixed up her words and made such a fool of herself. Kathleen glanced at the floor — her cheeks burning.

What if she accidentally made a similar mistake during the spelling bee? Oh, why did she have to think about that now? She might spell her word backward or something — and this time it would be in front of the whole class.

Kathleen said a quick prayer, squared her shoulders, and faced the classroom. Freddie would go first — she was thankful for that. The first few rounds came and went without any of the difficulties or odd mistakes that Kathleen had feared. Soon the class was on the edge of their seats wondering what word would finally break the tie. Nobody noticed the slow tick-tock from the clock on the wall. All eyes were steadfastly focused on the front of the room.

"The next word will be 'stethoscope.' Freddie, it's your turn." Miss Brooklin nodded to Freddie, who confidently stood up to spell his word.

That would be an easy word for Freddie. His father was a doctor. Dr. Schmitt had used one when he checked up on Kathleen after the race. She never had explained to Dr. Schmitt or Freddie about the "doll dress pie." She should sometime, but it was far too embarrassing to bring up.

"Stethoscope, s-t-e-t-h-o-s-c-o-p-e, stethoscope."

The classroom became still.

"Correct." Miss Brooklin looked down at the paper she held in her hand and up at Kathleen.

Everyone's heads turned toward Kathleen. If she misspelled her word, Freddie would be the winner and go on to the citywide competition. The room grew quiet.

"The next word is 'xylophone,' " Miss Brooklin announced.

Kathleen stood. She had studied that word with Papa, and she had made a point to remember it because it was so funny. But now, a sudden feeling of panic came over her, and she began to envision what the students' expressions would be if she spelled the word all mixed-up or backward. She could feel the whole classroom staring back at her. Kathleen saw Patricia smirk. She closed her eyes and tried to think. Normally, when she closed her eyes, she could picture exactly what a word looked like, but this time it didn't work. All she could see was Patricia's triumphant sneer. She tried to focus. It only worsened the problem — now all she saw were strange, mixed-up versions of the word like — loxphoney and phoneloxy.

Kathleen's Shaken Dreams

"Kathleen, you need to at least try," Miss Brooklin said gently.

Kathleen looked at her teacher and nodded anxiously. She closed her eyes.

Dear Lord, please help my mind to focus. Help me not to be distracted or intimidated.

Kathleen took a deep breath and straightened her shoulders.

"Xylophone, x-y-l-o-p-h-o-n-e, xylophone."

"Correct," Miss Brooklin nodded in approval.

Freddie misspelled the next word, gladiolus, by one letter, spelling it with an "e" instead of an "i."

"Kathleen, would you please spell 'gladiolus,' " Miss Brooklin said.

Kathleen stood and confidently spelled the word.

There was a long pause. Kathleen looked questioningly at Miss Brooklin. Had she spelled it wrong? Finally Miss Brooklin smiled.

Kathleen flew through the back door into the kitchen. "Mama! Papa! I did it. I won the spelling bee. I'm going to the citywide competition next month."

Mama and Papa sat at the kitchen table. Papa was holding a newspaper, and they were intently listening to the radio. Slowly they looked up, but they stared at her as if they didn't even see her.

"I'm serious—this is not a joke. I won! My name is going to be published in the newspaper. That means it will be broadcast on the radio. Can you believe that?"

They still didn't seem to notice. The radio was loud, and it was hard to hear the reporter over the crackling static.

"Mama, did you hear me?" asked Kathleen, beginning to wonder what was so important in the news.

"What did you do, dear?" Mama asked. She seemed pale.

"I won the spelling bee! Freddie and I were tied and then he messed up and I spelled gladiolus. I almost misspelled xylophone, but thanks to you, Papa . . ."

Papa was looking at the newspaper again and didn't look up. Kathleen felt hurt. It was as if she hadn't even come into the room. Mama kept looking from Kathleen to the paper in Papa's hand and then back again as if she was trying to listen but was too distracted to really focus.

"Many are calling today's events Black Tuesday," Kathleen heard the news reporter say. "Wall Street is claiming that things will improve, but there is an eerie feeling surrounding this whole unexplainable event. The mood of the people on Wall Street seems desperate — as if this was the end of the world."

"What's the matter? What's going on? What are you reading?" Kathleen peered over Papa's shoulder and read the headlines written in bold lettering.

STOCK MARKET CRASH
LEAVES MILLIONS PENNILESS AND HOPELESS

Kathleen's Shaken Dreams

What did that mean? Papa's face was ashen, and Mama kept gently squeezing his arm, like she was consoling him. They both seemed worried. Kathleen backed out of the room, an uneasy feeling growing in the pit of her stomach. Something must be terribly wrong.

Later that night, Kathleen leaned her ear against the crack in her bedroom door, trying to hear what her parents were saying.

"I'm sorry I've been so sober, Claire. It's just that I sense that the effects of this crash will have serious . . ."

Kathleen couldn't hear the rest of the sentence. She pressed her ear harder against the door. Mama and Papa had stayed in the living room talking much later than usual. At first Kathleen had lay in bed trying not to pay attention to their muffled voices, but then her curiosity had gotten the best of her. She had to know what was going on. It all seemed so strange — her papa's serious, somber behavior and her mama's obvious concern about the grim headlines in the news. To Kathleen the newspaper was the same as it was every day, but for some reason today's headlines made everything feel uncertain, and Kathleen was determined to figure out why.

"Yes, dear, I do understand the importance of the stock market, but I don't see how a bad business day in New York City could affect you and your job here in Fort Wayne, Indiana. It just doesn't seem possible."

There it was, a tenseness in her mama's voice that made Kathleen's heart afraid.

"I know it must seem odd that I'm so concerned, but if you only saw the look in Mr. Williams' face when he heard the news . . ." Papa's voice faded out again. Kathleen held her breath, trying not to miss any more words. Mr. Williams was the owner and president of the construction company that Papa worked for.

"The only thing I can make of it is that he must have lost everything," Papa said. "Mr. Williams often boasted of the money he was making in the stock market. I'm afraid he's invested a great deal of his personal and company money in the market."

Papa wasn't making any sense. What did "invested in the market" mean and how in the world did a market crash?

"As the accountant for his construction company, I don't know how long he can stay afloat . . . or how much longer he will be able to pay an accountant for that matter."

"Let's just hope and pray that the market improves, James," Mama said gently.

"We need to do lots of praying. As you know, Claire, we have just spent our savings paying off the mortgage on the house and buying our new Chevrolet, so if I was to lose my job now . . ." Kathleen strained to hear what Papa was saying.

"James, I will start economizing immediately. I can save on the grocery bill, and we can cut the children's allowances in half."

"No. We don't need to do that yet — I don't want to alarm the children. It would be best to keep things the same as much as we can."

There were a few more words that Kathleen couldn't quite catch, and then the house lights began to go out one by one. That meant they were heading to their room. Kathleen turned back toward her bed. There was nothing more she could do to figure out what was going on.

That night Kathleen tossed and turned, trying in vain to sleep. She tried dreaming about traveling to far-away lands, but that only made things worse.

If Papa lost his job, and they were out of money, would that mean they'd have to live in a mud-floored hut like the poor people in faraway countries that they supported through missions? Or worse, would they have a house at all?

Kathleen had never even thought about not having a home, food, and clothing. Everything was always provided for her, but she had read stories of princesses suddenly being reduced to poverty and slave labor.

If that could happen to a princess in a castle, then it could happen to her. And what about her allowance? If she didn't have that, how would she buy Christmas and birthday gifts for her family? She thought of the toy boat that she'd been saving her pennies for. It would be such a perfect gift for Richard. And there was the cute teapot for her mama that she'd been saving up for ever since last Christmas. She almost had enough money to buy it, but now she might not be able to.

Kathleen's imagination went wild. The more she thought about the grim possibilities that lay ahead, the more terrified she became. She prayed and asked Jesus to soothe her fears and felt better for a moment, but then another uncertain thought came. Soon her doubts doubled until finally she couldn't stand it any longer. She had to talk to someone. Kathleen slipped out of bed and padded down the hall to her parents' room.

Stormy Horizons

And we know that in all things God works for the good of those who love him, who have been called according to his purpose.
ROMANS 8:28

"Mama, are you awake?" Kathleen whispered as she pushed open her parents' bedroom door. She could hear her mama roll over in the dark and start to wake up.

"Yes, dear, what is it?"

"Could—could I talk to you a minute? I can't sleep."

"Of course. Go back to your room, so we don't wake your papa, and I'll be right there."

Kathleen had just climbed back in bed when Mama followed through the door. She turned on her bedside lamp and sat next to Kathleen. Though her mama's presence made Kathleen's heart more settled, there still was an enormous amount of uneasiness brewing inside.

"Mama, are we going to go hungry and have to live in a dusty hut like the people from Africa that we send money to?"

"What? You poor dear! Where on earth did you come up with that idea?"

"Because of that crash thing. You know, the market that crashed—that the newspaper was talking about. I mean, if Papa really does lose his job . . ."

Mama looked at Kathleen and raised her eyebrows in question. Kathleen's cheeks grew warm. She sat up in bed.

"I have a confession. I—I was listening to your conversation earlier—I had to know why you and Papa were so serious. I know it's not right to eavesdrop, but my curiosity got the better of me."

"Yes, it did, and I think you're beginning to understand why unchecked curiosity can get you in all sorts of unnecessary trouble. Now your head is full of all kinds of things that you should not have to worry about." Mama sighed. "Kathleen, there is a reason why you are not supposed to listen in on other people's conversations."

"I know, Mama, and I'm very sorry."

Mama pulled Kathleen up into her lap like she did when she was a little girl and whispered in her ear, "I'm not upset, except that I am sorry you have to worry about any of this." Mama paused, but Kathleen didn't mind. She was happy to rest in the comfort of her mama's arms.

"Perhaps it is best that you understand what is going on. You are twelve years old now, and I think it is about time you started being involved in more adult conversation."

Kathleen's Shaken Dreams

It warmed Kathleen's heart to know that her mama wanted to treat her like a young lady, but at that precise moment she felt like a little girl who just wanted her mama to make everything okay. She wished that Mama would kiss her forehead and tell her that nothing was wrong and that everything would turn out okay. Instead, it seemed that Mama was acknowledging there really was a possibility that Papa might lose his job as a result of this whole crash thing.

"Is Papa really going to lose his job?" Kathleen asked.

Mama brushed out of Kathleen's eyes the strand of red hair that stubbornly got loose because of her cowlick. "We don't know that yet. There is so much to explain to you—I don't really know where to start. Perhaps Papa can tell you a little more about the stock market. But for now all you need to remember is that when given adult information, you must also choose to respond in a mature way. You must have complete faith and trust in your Heavenly Father, and act in a God-honoring manner."

"How do I do that? I'm already a Christian and I read my Bible and try my best to follow Christ's example. What else is there to do?" Kathleen yearned to have the same peace and confidence reflected in her mama's eyes and voice.

"Well, each and every day you have opportunities in life to choose to trust Jesus—in small as well as large life decisions and experiences. You have the opportunity to grow in your relationship with Him and find out what a faithful friend He is. Kathleen, even if your papa was to lose his job, your Heavenly Father would still be there, and in His Word He has promised that He will provide for His children. I've learned never to dread hardship, because it is during those times that our faith is stretched and we grow closer to the Lord."

Kathleen nodded with a sleepy yawn. Her mama's words brought consolation to her soul. She spoke about her trust in God with such peace and joy that Kathleen couldn't help but feel that she too could have peace in her heart.

"There is so much to tell you, Kathleen, but for now rest in the knowledge that nothing can ever happen that your Heavenly Father does not allow. And He has promised never to leave you or forsake you."

The next morning before school, Kathleen searched the morning paper to see if they had published her name as the winner of the spelling bee. She finally found it, but the grim-sounding news about Wall Street squelched most of the thrill. Then on the way to school, it seemed that everywhere she turned on the streets people were selling newspapers and talking about the stock market crash. She thought a lot about what Mama had told her the night before about trusting God and not being fearful. Kathleen tried all day to simply trust without anxiety, but by the end of the afternoon she felt a sick, restless feeling in the bottom of her stomach. She couldn't wait for school to be over so she and Lucy could talk in the solace of her tree house.

"Is your father concerned about losing his job too?" Kathleen asked as they climbed up the rope ladder into the tree house.

"Why would my father worry about that? He's the president of International Farm Implements." Lucy sounded a little surprised at the question.

"Because of the stock market crash."

"Oh, that." Lucy shrugged as she got out her mending basket and started sewing the hem of a new dress she was making for her doll. "I heard my dad saying something to my mom about it, but he didn't sound too concerned. I don't really understand what happened, do you?"

"Papa tried to explain it to me this morning, but it still doesn't make much sense." Kathleen got her sewing project out and threaded her needle. She and Lucy were making matching doll dresses. There was a long pause, and then Kathleen cocked her head to the side in thought. "All I can make of it is that a whole lot of people—like my dad's boss—lost lots of money. Some are concerned that it might have a bad effect on the economy." Kathleen smiled to herself, feeling grown up for using such adult words.

Lucy looked puzzled. "What's the economy?"

"Papa says it has to do with how much people are buying and selling. If the economy is good, everyone is

buying. This creates more jobs and in turn more money for people to spend. But if the economy is bad, people stop buying, which makes companies lose money, and then people lose their jobs. That is what might happen to Papa. You see, his boss invested and lost almost all his money in the stock market, and unless lots of people all of a sudden want to build new houses right now, Papa fears that the construction company will not have enough money to keep paying him."

"Oh! Th—that doesn't sound very good." Lucy looked concerned but mostly just confused.

"Yes, well, the market crash must be terrible, because this morning when I was listening to the *Chicago Morning Show* on the radio, the announcer reported that there was a rumor that some of the rich people in New York who lost all their money have gone as far as ending their lives by jumping off their high-rise office buildings."

Lucy stopped sewing. "That's terrible."

"Like they said, it could be just a rumor, but what they say for sure is that people are beyond desperate."

"I had no idea things were that bad," said Lucy.

"Yes, I was awfully afraid at first, but Mama says now that I'm older, I must learn to trust Jesus in the bigger things in life too. She told me that when our faith is stretched, our trust in God and our relationship with Him grows the most."

"That sounds so exciting! Not that I would ever want your dad to lose his job, but your mama is right—

even though things look bad, God will work it out for the best."

"That's what I've been telling myself all day. Only, I have found that it is easier to say it with confidence than it is to feel the same assurance in my heart."

"I know exactly how you feel. I cried and cried when my father's job moved him away from Michigan to Fort Wayne. I thought my whole life was ending." Lucy sighed at the memory, and then straightened her shoulders. "But, Peter showed me a verse in the Bible that promises that everything works together for good for those who love God. He told me that even when my future is unsure, I can be excited because I know God still has great things in store. Peter said it would be like a great mystery, and the only thing I had to do to enjoy the mystery was keep my eyes focused on the Lord, and I would be able to embrace the adventures that lay ahead. Peter said if I was always worrying about what might happen someday, or if I spent all my time wishing things were like they used to be, I would miss all the good things that God had for me today."

"That all sounds good, but I don't know if I could be excited about my dad losing his job." Kathleen looked doubtfully at her friend, but Lucy remained undaunted.

"That's almost exactly what I told Peter—especially when I found out that he would be staying at my grand-parents'. But, Kathleen, he was right! Don't you see? If I hadn't moved here, I would have never gone to the Monroeville Highland Games. And if Peter had been

there that day, I probably would not have run the footrace. And if I hadn't run, then I may not have ever met you. So you see, I'm sure that God will work everything out for the best."

Just then there was a bright flash that lit up the sky and the crack of thunder.

"That lightning looked dreadfully close," said Lucy.

Kathleen glanced out the window at the dark clouds forming overhead. "Looks like a bad storm. We better make a run for it!" Kathleen shivered and wrapped her hands around her arms as a cold gust of wind blew through their tree house causing the yellow curtains to flap helplessly in the window.

"A tree house is the last place to be in a thunderstorm." Lucy folded up her sewing and stuffed it into her basket.

"Quick, Lucy! Help me close the window shutters."

The girls hastily closed the shutters, gathered their belongings, and wrapped their coats tightly about them. Kathleen's mama had insisted she wear her maroon wool dress and heavy winter coat that morning, but Lucy's dress was made of much thinner-weight cotton, and she wore a lightweight jacket with no hood. Kathleen looked at Lucy's jacket and shook her head.

"Why don't you wear my coat? I'm afraid we're going to get soaked."

"No, it is my fault I'm wearing this. Mama told me the days were growing colder, but I'm so warm-natured I could not stand the thought of dressing warmly before the first snow. I'll just run quickly. That will keep me warm."

Before the girls reached the bottom step of the rope ladder, small drops of rain began to make little watermarks on their dresses. Kathleen felt a shiver of excitement. She loved the wind and rain—especially in the fall when the strong gusts would send thousands of shimmering autumn leaves flying through the air.

The wind picked up quickly and soon the droplets of rain turned into torrents of heavy showers. The rain pelted against their faces, and the girls had to squint as they ran.

"Are you all right?" Kathleen called out, fighting to be heard above the loud cracks of thunder. She noticed that Lucy was winded and lagging behind. Normally Lucy would be right behind or even neck and neck with Kathleen, but this time she seemed to tire quickly and her face looked unusually pale. Then Kathleen remembered that Lucy had complained about a sore throat that morning.

Kathleen's thoughts went back to her old girlfriend, Mary Fletcher. Fear clutched her heart. Mary was healthy, just like Lucy. Then last fall, when they were playing blindman's bluff during recess, Kathleen noticed that Mary had a slight cough. The next day she didn't come to school. At first, her teacher said it was nothing to worry about—just a slight cold. But Mary developed pneumonia. Then, just before Christmas, she died.

A lump formed in Kathleen's throat as she remembered the grief she had felt when Papa had told her the sad news.

Please, Lord, don't let Lucy get sick — I don't think I could bear to lose her.

Lucy's Illness

"Do not let your hearts be troubled. Trust in God . . ."
JOHN 14:1

Lucy came down with a cold just as Kathleen had feared. Dr. Schmitt said that it wasn't too serious, but just in case, he prohibited any visitors. Each morning, as Kathleen walked by the Meiers' house on the way to school, she looked longingly at Lucy's bedroom window. She couldn't believe that her dear friend was so sick that she couldn't even talk to her.

Richard tried his best to cheer Kathleen on their walks to school, but nothing seemed to help.

Kathleen struggled to concentrate in school. Lucy's empty seat was a constant reminder of her illness.

Freddie stopped and talked to her during their lunch break. "I'm sure your friend will be back in class soon. You know my papa—he's always taking precautions just in case."

Kathleen thanked him for his effort to encourage her—she really did appreciate it. But it was the "just in case" scenario that shot pangs of fear into the depths of her heart.

Throughout the following week, it was hard for Kathleen to focus on her homework. She refused to go to the tree house until Lucy was well enough to go with her. It would be too lonely, and she would think of Lucy far too much to keep her mind on her studies. Kathleen rarely even thought about the stock market now that Lucy was sick. Even though Mama and Papa would talk about people who lost everything because of the crash, it really didn't seem to affect their family. Life continued as normal. The only thing that was different was Lucy's absence, which Kathleen felt keenly.

"I don't know how you'll win that citywide spelling bee if you keep staring out the window all afternoon," Papa said about a week after Lucy had taken ill. "I'll tell you what. Why don't you let me quiz you?"

"Oh, Papa, would you?" Kathleen's face broke into a smile for the first time in what seemed like years. She was convinced that her papa was the smartest man in town, and she loved it when he helped with her homework.

The next day when Kathleen returned from school her mama told her that Lucy's mother had called.

"Mrs. Meier wanted to know if you would like to visit Lucy today. Dr. Schmitt said that she is on the mend and is allowed to have visitors."

Kathleen's Shaken Dreams

Kathleen dropped her books on the table. "Really? Mama, can I go over right now? I promise I will get all my homework done this evening—no, I'll even bring it with me—Lucy will want to know what we're learning so she won't get too far behind." Kathleen's words stumbled over each other.

Mama laughed. "I'm so glad to see a smile on your face again. Yes, you may go."

Kathleen started for the door, turned back, and grabbed her books.

"Don't worry about coming home for supper," Mama called as she ran out the door. "Mrs. Meier invited you to eat with them."

"Thank you! I promise I will remember my manners and behave in a ladylike fashion." Kathleen waved as she ran down the driveway.

Kathleen's hand shook with excitement as she knocked on the Meiers' front door. She took a deep breath and waited for some time without any sign of life from within—not even the rustle of footsteps coming down the large wooden staircase.

Should she knock again? Their house was so huge, maybe they had not heard her.

She raised her fist to knock again when she heard footsteps approaching from behind. It was Lucy's older sister Deanna.

"Hello, Kathleen! Are you here to check on Lucy?"

"Yes, ma'am. I am." Kathleen blushed. She quickly smoothed the wrinkles from the waistline of her blue

110

cotton dress, straightened her lace-trimmed collar, and then brushed the curl that her stubborn cowlick always planted across her face. Deanna was a beautiful girl and always looked perfect in her nurse's uniform. Next to her Kathleen felt like an awkward girl whose clothing could never keep up with her constant growth spurts.

"Oh, my. Please don't call me ma'am—that makes me feel primeval. I came straight home from work to check up on Lucy myself. Let's go in together." Deanna smiled sweetly at Kathleen as she pushed open the heavy wooden door. Kathleen watched Deanna as she gracefully led the way into the house. Her blonde curls were pinned back, framing her face perfectly beneath her nursing cap. Under her arm she held a book and several magazines. It made Kathleen wonder if she loved reading as much as Lucy.

Soon they were up the two flights of stairs and at Lucy's bedroom door.

"Go ahead, Kathleen. I'll check on Lucy later after I change into a more comfortable dress," Deanna said as she started to unpin the bobby pins that kept her hat in place. "I'm sure the two of you have a lot of catching up to do."

"Thank you." Kathleen watched Deanna walk down the hall to her room. She was almost afraid to knock on Lucy's door. How sick would she look? Would Lucy be sleeping? Would she be able to talk long without losing her strength? Kathleen didn't want to fatigue Lucy and

make her condition worse. Slowly, Kathleen opened the door.

"There you are! I've been waiting for you all day." Lucy's cheerful voice eased Kathleen's fears.

"I've missed you miserably! I came as soon as I got home from school." Kathleen hugged Lucy and then settled into a wicker chair beside her bed.

Lucy was not only wide awake, but she was reading *Pilgrim's Progress*. She looked much better than Kathleen had imagined. Her cheeks weren't as rosy as they normally were, but they did have color in them, and her eyes sparkled with life.

Even though the last week and a half had seemed like an eternity, it didn't take long for the girls to get caught up.

"How is your father's job?" Lucy asked as soon as there was a lull in the conversation.

"His job? Oh! It's going well—I mean he still has it," Kathleen shrugged. "I haven't had time to think about it. I've spent too much time praying that you'd get better."

Lucy smiled. She propped herself up to a sitting position so she could look Kathleen in the eyes.

"Thank you," she said. "I know your prayers are working. Can you believe that the last time we talked was in the tree house the day after the spelling bee? I've had a lot of time to think, and for some reason that conversation about trusting Jesus to work everything out for good kept coming back to my mind. At first, I had

a hard time finding any good in being confined to my bed and missing school. Then I decided to pray that God would help me to see the good in it. And guess what happened?"

"You started getting better?"

"Nope, that didn't happen until a few days later. Peter just happened to call, and Mama told him I was sick. My grandparents don't have electricity or a telephone line at the farm, so we only get to talk when Peter goes to town for supplies. That only happens about once a month, if that often. But when Peter heard that I was sick, he promised that he'd make the trip to town more often. Since then, we've talked every single day."

"Really? He must love you an awful lot." Kathleen wondered what it would be like to have an older brother who cared for her like that.

"I told him all about you, Kathleen, and it helped me not miss both of you quite as much." Lucy leaned over and picked up her doll, Belle, off the wicker nightstand next to her bed. "Every time I looked at Belle, I would think of a fun memory we've had together in your tree house."

"Like when your mother sent that wonderful apple strudel and we had a tea party?" Kathleen's stomach growled. "Speaking of apple strudel, whatever your mother is baking downstairs is sure making me hungry. It smells wonderful!"

"It's a Black Forest cake, one of her specialties. Mama's been trying to coax my appetite since I've been

on the mend. She's made all sorts of tasty goodies." Lucy licked her lips and patted her stomach. "It's sure been working. I think I only have a couple more pounds to gain and I'll be as good as new."

Soon all sorts of delicious smells from the kitchen filled Lucy's room. By the time Mrs. Meier announced that it was dinnertime, both the girls' stomachs were growling heartily.

Lucy's father took her arm and led her downstairs to the dinner table. Kathleen placed a pillow on Lucy's chair back and settled into the seat next to her. It was the first time Lucy had eaten with the family since she'd fallen ill.

"Shall we bless the food?" Mr. Meier asked with his distinct German accent. Once everyone was situated, he bowed his head. "Dear Father in Heaven, we thank You for this food that You have abundantly blessed us with and tonight we want to especially thank You that Lucy is recovering from her illness, and we do humbly ask for her continued healing." Mr. Meier paused and then the rest of the family joined in as they recited their traditional family prayer.

"Come, Lord Jesus, be our guest and let Thy gifts to us be blessed. Amen."

Kathleen's heart filled with joy and gratitude to God as she looked around. Lucy still looked weak, but she was healing, and the Meier family was so kindhearted and loving that she truly felt as if she were eating in her own home.

Deanna, who was sitting across the table from Kathleen, broke the silence. "Rose darling, why don't you pass the potato salad to Kathleen so we can get started? I worked up quite an appetite at the hospital today."

"Did you get many new patients today?" Rose asked as she held the salad bowl so Kathleen could serve herself. Kathleen noticed for the first time that Rose and Deanna had the same little dimple in their chins.

"Not too many, but I did help deliver two new babies." Deanna tucked one of her blonde curls that had escaped from her bobby pin behind her ear. "And trust me, it kept me on my toes. But being able to witness the miracle of birth is my favorite part of being a nurse."

"There is nothing sweeter than the sound of a new babe coming into this world." Mrs. Meier smiled as she ladled scrumptious-looking German meatballs onto a bed of steaming spaetzle.

"And you would know too, considering that you've had six of us." Helen laughed as she passed the red cabbage dish to Mr. Meier. Her blue eyes always had a sparkle in them, just like Lucy's.

"Six children?" Kathleen questioned. They all looked so much alike, maybe she had miscounted. She looked around the table and counted Lucy and three sisters. "I know that Peter is missing, but who—oh yes, that's right, you have an older sister who is—married?"

"Yes, her name is Dottie," Lucy said. "She and Joseph, her husband, will be joining us at my grandparents' farm for Thanksgiving. Oh! And did I tell you

Kathleen's Shaken Dreams

Peter may be able to come home with us after Thanksgiving? Then you can finally meet him."

"I would like that very much," Kathleen said as she buttered her dinner roll.

Dinner continued with much lively chatter. After Mrs. Meier's delicious chocolate cake was served, the two girls retired to the living room to do homework.

All too soon the cuckoo clock beside the fireplace mantel announced it was time to go home by playing a lovely alpine tune as little figurines dressed in traditional German costumes danced around in a circle. Then a little bird popped out crying, "cu-coo, cu-coo, cu-coo," eight times. Kathleen paused from her math problem to watch. Her time with Lucy had gone too quickly. She hoped it wouldn't be too long until she saw her again.

The days flew by and the November winds grew steadily colder. The last few leaves that clung to the trees seemed to whisper of the coming winter snows. Kathleen always looked forward to this time of year. She loved the anticipation of the first snow that would wrap the world around her in a silvery white blanket. Snow meant sledding, ice-skating, snowball fights, and best of all, it meant Christmas was just around the corner. When Kathleen noticed a cold gust of wind blowing the last of the maple leaves off the big tree in their front yard, she breathed deeply of the crisp fall air and cried, "Fall is almost over and Christmas is just around the corner."

Her mama laughed and reminded her that it wasn't even Thanksgiving yet.

Lucy was back in school now, and for the next couple of weeks, life continued with no major changes. Kathleen's parents hardly ever talked about the stock market or the economy, and she was comforted that her papa still had his job. But occasionally she would overhear someone at school saying that their father or uncle or their father's friend had lost his job, and it always made her uneasy. She would think back to the month before when the stock market crashed and she overheard her parents' grim conversation. Her parents never discussed financial issues with her, but she often wondered how things were really going at her papa's job and if his boss's company was getting enough work to keep paying him. Since she and Richard were still getting their allowance, she decided the situation must not be too bad.

Each time Kathleen began to think too much about it, she would remember her conversation with Lucy about trusting Jesus in all things and then she would scold herself for worrying. Besides, the citywide spelling bee was coming up, and Kathleen knew she must focus all her energy on studying.

The big day finally came. It was the week before Thanksgiving. Once again, Kathleen was beside herself with anxiety. Papa, Mama, Richard, and Lucy all came to cheer for her.

"Papa," said Richard as they climbed out of the car, "I wish you would have let me stay home and listen to

Kathleen's Shaken Dreams

Kathleen's competition on the radio. I wanted to hear Miss Kathleen McKenzie's voice on a real live radio."

"That would have been fun, but aren't you glad you can be here to show your support?" Papa tousled Richard's hair.

Kathleen's heart tingled with excitement as they walked across the parking lot. She couldn't believe her voice would be broadcast across the city on the radio. *Dear Lord, please help me to be humble and focused, remembering that I am here to glorify You with the gifts You've given me.*

The competition was held in their school auditorium. Kathleen and the other students sat on chairs lined up facing the audience. It was surprising to see how many people showed up. The auditorium was packed with standing room only at the back.

The school principal, Mr. Becker, began by welcoming the students from around the city and listing the respective schools they represented. He briefly went over the schedule of events and then wished everyone well. Just when Kathleen thought Mr. Becker had finished his speech, he announced that the winners would go on to the state competition in Indianapolis and, if they were successful, to the national competition.

"Nationals will be held in Washington, D.C.," Mr. Becker said. "The statewide winners in each grade level will be invited on a tour of the capital city, including a special tour of the White House and other historic sights near the D.C. area. Best of all, the national win-

ners will possibly have the opportunity to meet Herbert Hoover, the President of the United States."

Kathleen could not believe what she was hearing. She searched the crowd for her papa to see if he had heard. He was sitting near the middle aisle and wore a wide grin on his face. Kathleen knew what he was thinking. He loved history. He had told her many stories of the Founding Fathers and the wonderful monuments that could be seen at the nation's capital. Kathleen had always dreamed of the day she might go there. Now was her chance. Papa would so love it, if she could go. *Please, Lord, let me win . . . of course, only if it's Your will. But please help me to do my best. It would mean so much to Papa. Thank You, dear Lord. Amen.*

Triumphs and Trials

*Enter his gates with thanksgiving and his courts with praise;
give thanks to him and praise his name.*

PSALM 100:4

The auditorium fell silent. Throughout the great hall, the attention of every man, woman, and child was focused on the stage, watching the girl at the front. Kathleen looked down the row of seventh grade students. When the competition had first started she counted thirty-six contestants; now there were only four. Kathleen wiped her clammy hands on her dress and tried to remain calm.

"Sally Brunswick, please spell 'asceticism,'" Miss Brooklin said.

Looking bewildered, the poor girl stood up and began. "Asceticism, a-s-i-t . . . I mean, a-s-e-c-t-i-s-e-s-m."

"Incorrect."

Kathleen grimaced. She felt sorry for the girl as she watched Sally slowly walk off the stage. She looked terribly disappointed.

Miss Brooklin looked at the next boy on the row. "Robert Thornton, would you please spell 'intelligible.' "

Kathleen was up next. She hoped she would get a word like Robert's and not like Sally's.

Robert missed his word.

"This is it," Kathleen whispered under her breath. "Dear Lord, please help me to focus."

"Kathleen McKenzie, please spell 'pseudonym.' "

Kathleen stood and straightened her shoulders without any hesitation. "Pseudonym, p-s-e-u-d-o-n-y-m, pseudonym."

"Correct. Miles Goforth, please spell 'luxuriance.' "

Kathleen sat back down. She held her breath. Miles was the last competitor in the seventh grade competition. If he missed this word, it would mean that she was the winner and would represent Fort Wayne, Indiana, at state.

"Luxuriance, l-u-x-u-r-i-a-n-s-e."

"Incorrect." Miss Brooklin faced the audience. "Will you please join me in congratulating Miss Kathleen McKenzie, winner of our seventh grade citywide spelling bee."

The auditorium burst into cheers and clapping. Kathleen could feel her cheeks growing hot, and she knew she must be blushing. She whispered a prayer of thanks to the Lord. Kathleen could not wait until the eighth graders were finished so she could celebrate with her family and Lucy.

Kathleen's Shaken Dreams

"I knew you could do it!" Papa said as soon as the competition ended. He scooped her up into a big hug.

"I got a little nervous when they asked you to spell 'appendicitis,'" said Mama, "but Papa just squeezed my hand and assured me that you'd do just fine. He was right." Mama beamed. Her deep blue eyes shone with pride.

Kathleen put her arm around Lucy, who had been standing off to the side, allowing the family to congratulate her first.

"I was so nervous," Kathleen said. "I can't wait to get home and retreat to the tree house. I have so much to think about, and we have so much to plan before our trip to D.C."

"Trip to D.C.?" Lucy looked surprised.

"Well, I wouldn't dream of going without you!"

"Aren't we counting our chickens before they hatch?" Mama said. "You haven't won state yet, have you?"

Kathleen knew what Mama was trying to do — bring her back to reality in her gentle, fun-loving way. "I know . . . but I have over two weeks to prepare, and I plan to spend every spare moment doing just that."

"I'll even help drill you!" said Richard, skipping alongside his big sister as they walked to the car. "That is, if I can read your big spelling words."

"That's the spirit!" Papa tousled Richard's hair.

Thanksgiving Day came and this year Pastor McCarthy and his wife were joining the McKenzie family for dinner. Kathleen was responsible for making the pies. She had been up since dawn peeling apples for the Dutch apple pie and carving out the rich flesh of a plump pumpkin for the spiced pumpkin pie. While she worked, Kathleen studied her spelling words. As she peeled, she paused to brush a strand of her red hair out of her face. She was glad she had shelled the nuts for the pecan pie the night before.

It was nearly noon, and she still had to roll out the pastry dough and shape the crusts. She didn't know if she'd ever be as efficient as Mama in the kitchen. All morning Mama whisked about, making cranberry sauce, sweet potato casserole, wild rice, dressing for the turkey, and fluffy dinner rolls, and stuffing the turkey with all sorts of rich spices. It was a wonder she managed to cook so much in such a short amount of time.

In years past, Mama had helped Kathleen with the pies, but this year she had announced, "I think it's time you start managing on your own. You've been baking the same pies each year since you were eight years old. Now you're a young lady—and, if I remember correctly, it was not too long ago that you won the baking contest with your blueberry pie."

At first Kathleen was pleased that Mama had entrusted her with so much responsibility, but as the morning flew by and as she reflected on her previous cooking catastrophes over the years, she felt slightly overwhelmed at the thought of making apple, pumpkin, pecan, and sweet potato pies, all before supper. However, Kathleen chose to take her mama's wise counsel just to focus on the next thing. Before she knew it, the kitchen was full of the rich, sweet-smelling aroma of baking pies. Much to her relief, Kathleen only ruined the pecan pie by accidentally placing three tablespoons of cornstarch in the filling rather than three teaspoons.

When Mama looked up from basting the turkey and saw what Kathleen had done, she said, "It's a slight mistake when reading the recipe, and easy to do, but a disastrous one — it is the difference between a pleasant texture and a rubbery one. But take heart, when I was your age, I started a kitchen fire while trying to fry doughnuts." Mama laughed and shook her head as she reflected on the memory. "We'll just throw this one out. All your other pies look marvelous."

The young pastor and his new bride arrived as planned. Papa and Pastor McCarthy both loved history and spent most of dinner telling exciting accounts of the Pilgrims and other forefathers that had founded America. Kathleen loved to listen to them. But when they started discussing the Bill of Rights and the constitutionality of the suffrage movement, she found herself wishing she was educated enough to understand every detail of their discussions. When she got to Washington, she was going to visit lots of museums and see these great documents firsthand. Then maybe she'd understand their discussion about the suffrage movement.

Later that evening, as she and Richard washed the dishes, Kathleen smiled as she thought about how happy Lucy must be in Michigan with her brother and grandparents. Kathleen envisioned what it must be like to spend Thanksgiving on a farm without modern conveniences like electric lights, indoor plumbing, and a telephone. She remembered spending several Christmases at Grandma and Grandpa McKenzie's and Uncle John's farm near Archbold, Ohio, but it had been so long ago. She had only a faint recollection of doing fun things like pumping water from a well and watching Grandma Maggie take sugar cookies out of a huge wood-burning stove that heated the whole kitchen as it cooked.

"Stay away from old Mary Washington. She's so hot she's likely to burn a hole right through your dress and scorch your wool bloomers," Grandma Maggie had said as she patted her stove affectionately. Kathleen had thought it kind of funny that her grandma named her stove until she got a little older and was able to read the brand name "Mary Washington" on the front panel of the oven. And it didn't dawn on Kathleen until a few years later that the stove couldn't have been quite as hot as Grandma Maggie always warned or else it would have burned Grandma Maggie too. At any rate, old Mary Washington produced the best sugar cookies Kathleen had ever tasted. That was one thing she would never forget about the farm.

There were a few things she wanted to forget, like the time her cousin Bruce locked her in the outhouse.

Kathleen's Shaken Dreams

Afterward, Uncle John had taken Bruce to the wood-shed for his little prank. Kathleen had not really under-stood the meaning of being taken to the woodshed at the time, but she did notice an immediate change in Bruce's behavior.

Kathleen had only slight memories of her cousins Alex and Lindsay. And little Robby hadn't even been born yet. Alex, the oldest, was tall, lanky, and red-headed. She remembered once when a mother cow had charged her, Alex had swung Kathleen up on his shoul-der and scolded the cow as if it were a child. It had amazed her because she had been so frightened and he hadn't been the least bit scared of it.

Lindsay was the only girl in the family and two years older than Kathleen. All Kathleen could remember of her was how she hid behind her mama's skirt, only dar-ing to peek out occasionally—her big brown eyes wide with wonder. Aunt Elizabeth had laughed and said, "She's a chatterbox when you get to know her. It's just that we don't get a lot of visitors here at the farm."

Of all her relatives, Aunt Elizabeth was the one that Kathleen could not ever forget. With the exception of her own mother, Elizabeth McKenzie was by far the sweetest, most beautiful woman Kathleen had ever met.

Kathleen smiled as she thought about Uncle John. She had thought Papa was proud of his Scottish heritage, until she met him. He loved to talk of Scottish history and went as far as naming all his sons after great Scottish heroes. Alex was named after King Alexander III; Bruce

and little Robby were both named after Robert the Bruce, who fought for freedom from England with William Wallace. Kathleen remembered Papa reading a letter from her uncle shortly after Robby was born. "A man who had the courage and strength to win Scotland's freedom from England at such great odds—he is worth having two sons named after him."

Kathleen shook her head. Papa was proud of their heritage, but Uncle John was passionate about it. She washed the last plate and gave it to Richard. Mama and Papa came into the kitchen.

"Kathleen, Richard, now that our guests are gone, your papa and I wish to talk to you about an important matter." Kathleen searched her mama's face for any sign of what it might be. She hadn't noticed anything different in their behavior all day, but now there was something—something in her mama's tone of voice that caused her to wonder.

"No need to look so alarmed, my bonny lass." Papa placed a kiss on the top of Kathleen's head.

"That's right, no need for fear. Do you remember what I told you several weeks ago about trusting the Lord?" Mama said, smiling gently.

"Yes, but what is it? Is something wrong?" Kathleen searched their faces for a clue.

Papa cleared his throat. "Yesterday, I was informed that the company I work for will be going out of business. I'll be out of a job at the end of the week. But, as this is Thanksgiving Day, your mama and I have had a

good reminder of how much we have to be grateful for. If God could take care of the Pilgrims in a wild, untamed land, He is definitely capable of meeting our needs here in Fort Wayne, Indiana."

Kathleen couldn't believe what she was hearing. What would happen to them if Papa didn't have a job?

12

Winter Storms

Your attitude should be the same as that of Christ Jesus:
Who, being in very nature God, . . . made himself nothing,
taking the very nature of a servant.

PHILIPPIANS 2:5-6

Kathleen slowly sat down at the kitchen table. Her thoughts spun in a million directions. One moment she felt sure that everything would be just fine, then the next, hundreds of questions flew through her mind.

She must not worry. The Lord would take care of them. But how could God take care of them if they didn't have any money?

Kathleen remembered the night she'd overheard her parents talking about the market crash. Now it seemed that her worst fears were realized. Her eyes filled with tears.

"Papa, will we have to live in a hut with dirt floors like the people we support in Africa?" she blurted out.

129

Kathleen's Shaken Dreams

"I would love to live in a hut in Africa. When do we go?" Richard jumped up, his eyes glowing with adventure.

"Richard, be quiet. You don't know what you are saying," said Kathleen. Lucy had to move when her father lost his job. Would this mean they would have to move too?

Papa tousled Richard's hair with his free hand. "Richard, you'd be ready for an adventure at the drop of a hat, wouldn't you? But, I'm afraid we'll not be going to Africa. In fact, I don't think we'll even have the pleasure of living in a hut." Papa grinned at Richard and then looked at Kathleen with concern.

"Kathleen, I think your fears have gotten the best of you this time. God truly could not have arranged a more merciful time for me to lose my job—the house is paid for, your mama and I own a brand-new car, and all I have to do is go find another job."

"Really? Do you mean everything is going to be okay?" Kathleen swallowed the lump that was growing in her throat and blinked back a few tears.

"Yes, dear. I don't know how the Lord will choose to provide, but I know that He will. Your reaction just now was a bit dramatic." Papa ran his finger down Kathleen's freckled nose. "Perhaps in the future it would be best to first try to find something to be grateful about in a situation instead of automatically jumping to the worst possible conclusion."

Kathleen pulled her handkerchief from her pocket and dabbed her eyes, feeling a little foolish. "You're

right, Papa; I am trying to be more grown up—it's just so hard not to worry sometimes—"

"Especially when you have such a huge imagination!" Richard said.

Mama motioned for Richard to hold his tongue, but Kathleen could tell she was trying to hide a smile.

Papa cleared his throat and looked deep into Kathleen's eyes. "I'm encouraged that you are trying to be more grown up—that can be a hard thing to do sometimes. So make sure you are seeking the Lord most of all and not trying to run the race of life in your own strength."

Kathleen listened intently to her papa's wise counsel. The compassion in his expression and tone of voice made Kathleen immediately feel like he understood. She knew that her faith would be tried in the days to come, but for now, Kathleen felt comforted that at least Papa could see that even though it was difficult, she was trying.

Sunday night after Thanksgiving Kathleen lay in bed awake. The wind howled outside and she snuggled deeper beneath her quilt. Kathleen could not wait until school tomorrow. She was anxious to hear all about Lucy's trip. She wanted to see if Peter had come home with her. Lucy had mentioned that he might be able to come home after Thanksgiving. Kathleen felt like she already knew Peter. After all, she spent a great deal of time with Lucy, who spent much of that time talking about Peter.

This week Kathleen would take a day trip to Indianapolis for the state spelling bee. Her stomach felt all twitchy whenever she thought about it. At times Kathleen thought she could no longer bear the anticipation. The spelling bee would not be until Friday though, so she would just have to wait.

She wished that Mama, Papa, and Lucy were going with her instead of Miss Brooklin and the principal. They would be able to listen on the radio and had all promised to pray for her, but it wouldn't be the same.

Kathleen fluffed her pillow and rolled over. Her papa had offered to help with the driving, but unfortunately with the teachers and three students that were representing the school, there was no extra room in the car.

When Kathleen awoke the next morning, the room seemed brighter than usual. She threw back the curtains. A snowstorm had blown in during the night, leaving a deep blanket of fluffy, gleaming snow.

"Hurray! Christmas is right around the corner!" She rushed to her dresser to dig out her bright red wool scarf and mittens. The cheerful color made Kathleen think about Christmas and the gifts she'd been saving for. She wondered if she would still get her one-dollar allowance at the end of the month. If Papa had not found a job by then, she might not. But she'd saved almost all of her allowance since last year. She thought she had about eight dollars — enough to buy wonderful gifts for her family.

When Richard and Kathleen reached the Meiers' on their way to school, Lucy was waiting at her mailbox. Kathleen only had to take one look into Lucy's troubled eyes to see that Peter must not have been able to come home with them.

"What happened? Why couldn't Peter come?" Kathleen gave Lucy a big hug.

Richard yanked on Kathleen's coat sleeve. "Excuse me. I want to get to school a little early. The guys are having a huge snowball fight. May I run ahead?"

"Okay—but be careful!" Kathleen called after him as he raced around the corner.

Lucy squeezed Kathleen's hand. "I really have nothing to complain about. Our trip truly was wonderful. It was so good to see Peter, but my grandparents still need him on the farm. Papa says Grandpa's health is failing fast . . ." Lucy's voice trailed off.

Kathleen decided she should tell Lucy about Papa losing his job to keep her from thinking of her grandpa and Peter. It worked. Lucy asked Kathleen question after question until they rounded the block just before school.

"Help!" someone called faintly.

Kathleen stopped. "What was that?"

Lucy grabbed Kathleen's arm. "Look! Over there." She pointed at a huge snowdrift several feet away. Two black boots stuck out of the top of it and they were kicking furiously. Kathleen heard the cry again. It came from the snowdrift, only this time she recognized the voice.

"Richard?" Kathleen gasped as she rushed toward the snowdrift.

"Hel-l-l-p?" The muffled cry sounded more like a sob.

"Lucy! It's Richard. Help me pull him out, quickly." Kathleen got as close as the snowdrift would allow, and she grabbed one leg while Lucy grabbed the other.

"Pull!" The girls tugged until poor Richard came sliding out, face down. His cheeks were red with cold. Tears streamed down his face. Kathleen wrapped him up in a big hug and tried to cover his shivering body with her coat.

"What in the world happened? Who did this awful thing?" she asked.

"J-Jake did it. He—he ch-chased me down and said that if I t-told anyone what he did, he'd cut a hole in the ice of the duck pond and leave me there till sp-spring," Richard blurted out between a mixture of sobs and shivers.

Her little brother's lips were blue, and he trembled with cold. All of a sudden her compassion for him turned into anger toward Jake. She could feel the heat growing from her heart and bursting into her veins.

"He will do no such thing! It is about time that big bully learned a thing or two. It is no man that goes around harming innocent little nine-year-olds." Kathleen was sure she had never been so upset in all her life.

"Yeah? What are you going to do?" a voice sneered nearby. Kathleen looked up to see Jake stepping out from behind a nearby woodpile. He was wearing a heavy winter coat and big black snow boots that made him appear twice as large as he was. Richard cowered closer to her side.

Kathleen's heart pounded in her ears. "It is about time you came out of your hiding place and faced your problems like a man!" Her voice sounded more controlled than she felt.

Jake tromped toward them, a scowl forming on his brow, his heavy boots thudding loudly on the packed snow.

Kathleen wondered if she had taken on a little more than she could handle. But then, almost at the same time, one of her Sunday school memory verses flashed in her mind. "God is my shield, saving those whose hearts are true and right," Kathleen whispered under her breath.

She straightened her shoulders and looked Jake straight in the eyes. "Why did you bury my brother in a snow bank? He could have gotten frostbite."

"Why did you have to come to the rescue so soon? You messed up all our fun," Jake sneered.

"*Our* fun?" Lucy asked. "Are there two of you?" Lucy glanced around and she looked as if she wanted to run.

"Yeah, my sidekick, Dan, is behind the woodpile. Anyway, Miss Kathleen McKenzie, what's this stuff I heard you say about teaching me a lesson? Looks like you and that kid brother of yours are the ones that need to learn a lesson or two." Jake patted a snowball that he grasped in his hand.

"If you throw that at any of us, I'll smash your face in the snow!" Kathleen said, hoping that Jake wouldn't hear the fear in her voice.

Jake laughed and hurled the snowball straight at Richard. Kathleen tried to step in front of her little brother to shield him, but it was too late. The frozen missile smacked Richard in the nose.

"Ouch!" Richard covered his face with his mittens. When he brought his hands down, there was blood smeared on his nose and mouth. The tears and sobs flowed freely.

Kathleen glared at Jake. Her heart raced. "How could you?" Kathleen shrieked as she raced toward Jake.

Jake looked surprised. He turned and tried to run away, but his foot slipped on a patch of ice, and he sprawled face-first in the snow.

Kathleen jumped on his shoulders, grabbed the back of his head, and rubbed his face in the snow. Jake whimpered. Kathleen released her grip.

"If you ever touch my little brother again — or any other child for that matter — you'll be sorry." Kathleen stood up, brushed the snow off her coat, and walked back to Lucy and Richard without looking back.

Kathleen pulled out her handkerchief and dabbed at the blood that was running down Richard's face. "Pinch your nose like this; it should stop the bleeding."

Richard did as he was told, his face full of amazement at what he'd just witnessed.

"I'll tell Miss Brooklin why you're late," said Lucy. "Actually, I think I'll go straight to the principal's office and tell him what happened — surely there is some way they can punish Jake and Dan for this."

Lucy gave Kathleen's hand a reassuring squeeze. They looked back where Kathleen had left Jake in the snow. He was sitting there crying and holding his forehead, which appeared to have hit a rock when he fell. Kathleen shook her head and put her arm around Richard's shoulders. "Come on, Richard! Let's get you home before you catch a cold."

Richard looked as if he wanted to stay and help his attacker.

Kathleen pulled on his arm. "He'll be alright," she said. "Dan is still hiding behind the woodpile. He will give Jake a hand just as soon as we leave."

Friday came at last and with it the state spelling bee in Indianapolis. Much to Kathleen's amazement and delight, she placed first out of all the seventh graders. The word that placed her at the top was 'deleterious.' Nationals would not be held until the spring, but Kathleen did not mind waiting. She was so overwhelmed at God's goodness to her. He had allowed her to win out of all the other students in the whole state of Indiana, and now she would have the opportunity to travel to Washington, D.C.

Kathleen's Shaken Dreams

All the way home from Indianapolis, she gazed at the one-dollar bill that her parents had given her for lunch money. Before the competition, she was too nervous to eat, and afterward Kathleen was far too elated to have an appetite. Even though she was hungry now, Kathleen was glad she had not used her money — she would much rather study the picture of George Washington on the dollar bill and dream about her upcoming visit to the capital city.

It was late when she arrived home and big, fat snowflakes fell heavily from the sky. Papa and Mama were waiting up for her. Kathleen could tell before she even got to the door — they had left the parlor lights on, something they only did for company, or on special occasions, like Christmas Eve. Kathleen smiled. Winning the state spelling bee was truly the best gift she could receive — it was like an early Christmas gift from Jesus. To her, the lights shone like a welcome beacon, streaming out the window and warming her heart. Kathleen immediately remembered what her papa had whispered in her ear just before she left for Indianapolis.

"Remember our McKenzie clan's motto, *Luceo non Uro* — 'we shine, not burn.' No matter what happens, don't forget to let Christ's love shine through you. It is all too easy to become so consumed in your own pride and selfish ambitions that you end up getting burned in the end. So, win or lose, remember who you are representing — Christ and your family name."

Winter Storms

Once again, Kathleen's heart filled with gratitude to the Lord for blessing her with a victory, and her parents would be so excited. She couldn't believe that her picture would be published in all of Indiana's prominent newspapers.

Dear Lord, I know that my talents come from You. Please let my attitude and actions bring glory to You. Help my heart not grow proud, so that I will shine for You.

An Unforgettable Christmas

"In everything I did, I showed you that by this kind of hard work we must help the weak, remembering the words the Lord Jesus himself said: 'It is more blessed to give than to receive.'"

ACTS 20:35

It snowed even more the next few weeks, making the scenery perfect for the Christmas season. Kathleen spent hours helping Mama bake cookies and other scrumptious treats. They made batch after batch of Grandma Maggie's famous Scottish shortbread, pecan tassies, gingerbread men, a whole assortment of sweet breads, and plenty of hot wassail—a delicious drink made with cider, spices, sugar, and baked apples.

Kathleen and Lucy's afternoons and evenings were filled with festive Christmas parties, ice-skating socials, and best of all, sledding adventures down at the riverbank near the tree house. The steep bank was the best sledding hill in town. Kathleen, Lucy, and Richard spent many happy hours sliding down it and shooting out across the hard frozen river.

Every morning when Kathleen woke, she grabbed her Bible from her nightstand and opened it. Before she read her devotion, she took out the newspaper clipping with her picture. It listed all the state spelling bee champions that she would be competing against at nationals. Then she asked God to help her be diligent in her studies and that her efforts would be blessed.

Now that Papa no longer worked at the construction company, he arrived home much later. He spent every day doing whatever part-time or odd jobs he could find, while searching for steady employment. Mama and Papa kept smiles on their faces. At first, Kathleen worried each evening when Papa announced that his job pursuit was unsuccessful, but he would add that tomorrow was a new day. "God's mercies are new each morning. The Lord knows what we need, and He'll provide in His timing," Papa would say with confidence.

As Christmas drew nearer, Kathleen counted her monthly allowance she had saved over the year, and then eagerly planned what she would buy for each family member.

Despite Papa being out of work, the collection of brightly wrapped packages grew rapidly under the tree. Kathleen was so eager to know what was in them. She thought about the gifts her parents had given last Christmas — a beautiful, miniature china tea set, the

prettiest lavender silk dress she had ever seen, and a silver, heart-shaped locket.

During the Christmas Eve service at church, Kathleen found it hard to focus on the sermon. She sat in the pew between her mama and papa, thinking about Richard's present. She could wrap his toy boat in one box and then put it inside another box and wrap that, and then put that box inside still another box. It would be such fun to see his face after opening one box, only to realize he had to open another.

"I'd like to close this evening's service," said Pastor McCarthy, "by wishing each of you a very Merry Christmas, and may we never forget that the true meaning of Christmas is to give rather than receive. Almost two thousand years ago the Christmas story began in a stable in Bethlehem where God gave the greatest gift ever — His Son Jesus — sent not to gain the world, but to lose His life on this earth in order that we might gain eternal life."

Kathleen sat straighter in her pew. She felt ashamed that she had not listened to more of Pastor McCarthy's sermon. God had given His only Son to die for her and all she could think about was Christmas morning. Being twelve was so hard.

Christmas morning Kathleen woke early. She barely had time to sit up in bed and stretch when Richard burst through the door.

An Unforgettable Christmas

"Merry Christmas! Let's go jump on Papa and Mama's bed and wake them up!" Richard said, his cheeks flushed with anticipation. He knew that Christmas Day was the only day of the year when that sort of behavior was permitted.

"I'm ready when you are." Kathleen laughed. Her hair was still wrapped up in curling rags that bounced when she moved.

"Charge!" Richard pretended to blow a fake bugle and the two stormed down the hall and burst into their parents' bedroom.

"Merry Christmas!" Kathleen cried cheerily as she and Richard jumped on their big bed.

"Happy New Year!" Richard hollered.

"Merry Christmas!" Papa yawned. He sat up in bed and stretched.

"Happy New Year to you, too." Mama rolled over and tried to flatten Richard's flyaway blonde hair.

Papa pulled his Bible off the nightstand, opened it, and began reading the Christmas story. As Papa explained how God became a little baby born in a stable, Kathleen imagined a great king sending his defenseless newborn son, whom he loved, to a far-off land—away from the protection and comforts of the palace. A king, who let his lowly tenant raise his only son, only to be crucified on a Cross in the end.

"God sent His Son," said Papa, "to show His great love for mankind. Jesus became the sacrifice for our sins. 'For without the shedding of blood there is no

remission of sin.' He humbled Himself to the point of becoming a man and willingly died on the cross for our sins. Christ set an example of love and humility by laying down His life for us. Our challenge is to follow His example daily in the small areas of life as well as the big areas."

After the Christmas story, the family moved to the parlor and gathered around the piano to sing "Hark the Herald Angels Sing," "Silent Night," and "The First Noel." As Mama played, Kathleen kept stealing glances at the brightly decorated Christmas tree that stood in the front parlor window. The morning sunlight streamed through the glass, lighting the silver tinsel until it sparkled brilliantly against the backdrop of the rich greenery and bright red cranberry garlands.

Finally, Papa said it was time. Each family member opened a gift while the others watched and waited their turn. Richard chose the big box from Kathleen first. Just as she suspected, he was delighted with the challenge of having to unwrap three boxes before getting to his wooden toy boat. When he saw it, he stared in awe and rubbed his hands down its smooth, gleaming red sides.

"Now *that* is a bonny boat," Papa said, playing up his Scottish accent.

"She sure is. Looks fast, too—I think I'll name her the *Bonny Kathy*. After you, Kathleen." Both Richard's smile and his naming the boat after her were the best thank-you Kathleen had ever received.

Next it was Kathleen's turn. She chose a gold package from her parents with a thin, silver bow on top. Her fingers shook as she unwrapped it. Inside rested a green clothbound book with a simple inscription embossed on the front: *Ben Hur* by Lew Wallace. Kathleen had heard the eighth grade literature class talk about the intriguing novel, but she had not read it.

"Thank you! I always enjoy a good book," Kathleen said, eagerly opening the cover and reading the inscription on the first page.

To our dear daughter, Kathleen,
*   May you always have a noble spirit that stands up for honor, truth, and justice. Most of all, may you ever be willing to humbly lay down your life for others.*
*   Love,*
*   Papa and Mama*
*   Christmas, 1929*

They continued to go around the room, opening presents, and soon it was Kathleen's turn. Once again she found a book wrapped beneath the pretty paper. Only this time it was an eighth grade American history book. Kathleen tried to smile gratefully, but she was confused. Why had they given her this? Eighth grade wasn't until next fall.

Then she remembered her upcoming trip to Washington, D.C. and assumed that her parents must have thought she would want to learn all the history she

could before then. But by the time Kathleen opened the next gifts and saw science, math, and geography books, there was no way to hide her disappointment. She looked at Richard. He too looked crestfallen as he gazed at his own assortment of schoolbooks.

"Why the downcast looks?" Papa asked. "I thought my children loved learning."

"Oh! I do, Papa. It's just, well—never mind. I can't wait to read *Ben Hur*. I hear it is a great book, and you wrote the loveliest inscription inside—I know I will always cherish it." Kathleen stood up and gave Papa a hug, trying her hardest to be sincerely grateful. After all, she was thankful for that book. The rest of them seemed like odd Christmas gifts. "I think I'll go to my room and start it right now. That is, unless you need my help in the kitchen." Kathleen turned to her mama. Her eyes burned and she blinked back tears that threatened to fall.

"Go along, dear," said Mama, putting her arm around Kathleen's shoulder. "Brunch will be ready at half past eleven, and by that time, you'll be a good ways into the book and can tell us what it's all about."

Kathleen thanked her mama and rushed to her room. She sat on her bed and gently opened her new book. Her eyes fell to the inscription written in her papa's handwriting. When she got to the last line, her eyes filled with tears as she read:

Most of all, may you ever be willing to humbly lay down your life for others.

146

An Unforgettable Christmas

She recalled the pastor's words the night before. "God gave the greatest gift ever in His Son Jesus, sent not to gain the world, but to lose His life on this earth in order that we might gain eternal life." Kathleen burst into tears. She felt bad for her ungrateful, self-centered attitude.

How could she ever learn to lay down her life for others? Here she was feeling sorry for herself because she got schoolbooks for Christmas—it wasn't as if God had called her to leave her home, her friends, everything she loved, to be a missionary in a faraway land. Besides, many children weren't fortunate enough to get a good education, let alone own their own books. It was just—last Christmas and her birthday had been so wonderful that she thought this Christmas would be too.

Kathleen buried her head in her pillow to muffle her sobs. Before long she heard a light knock on the door. She sat up and wiped the tears out of her eyes with her handkerchief. "Come in," she said, trying to sound like she hadn't been crying. The door opened. It was Mama.

"Kathleen? Do you mind if I talk to you?" Mama took off her kitchen apron and sat down on the bed. She brushed Kathleen's tangled red hair out of her eyes.

"Oh, Mama! I've been so dreadful. I know I should be grateful for my Christmas presents, but—but I'm not. And I'm awfully disappointed at myself for being so spoiled. I am sure that there are many children who would love to get an education but can't, and here I am crying because you and Papa gave me schoolbooks.

Kathleen's Shaken Dreams

How will I ever learn to lay my life down for others when I can't even be content with a Christmas gift?"

Mama laughed a little as she pulled her daughter into a big hug. "I'm glad you desire to be grateful and content with what God has given you. As for being frustrated and discouraged with yourself—well, that won't get you very far in life. Why don't you try spending your energy on having a better outlook, rather than focusing all your energy on why you don't have a good attitude?"

Kathleen nodded her head against her mama's shoulder.

"I will try my hardest. I promise."

"Now, as far as the schoolbooks go, I feel I should explain a little. As you know, your papa has been unable to find work for almost a month now. Thankfully, we paid off the house and car just before the stock market crash, but that means that when your papa lost his job, we had very little money left in the bank."

Kathleen looked into her mama's eyes trying to detect if what she was saying meant that Kathleen should have any cause to be concerned, but Mama's blue eyes were as peaceful and steady as always.

"No, dear, you need not worry. Remember, God supplies all the needs of His children. It is just that . . . well, so many different things could happen at this point—we do not always know how or when God will provide, but we know He will. However, finances are tight right now, so your papa and I thought that rather than having no Christmas gifts at all, we would spend the last of our savings on something that would benefit you and Richard in the future."

Though grateful for her mama's attempt to explain the family's financial circumstances, Kathleen spent many hours over the next few days trying to understand.

What did Mama mean when she said so many different things could happen? Was she saying that Papa might not find a job? Would they have to move somewhere else if he couldn't find a job in Fort Wayne?

The more Kathleen pondered, the more confused she became. Finally she consoled herself that she must be reading way too much into things.

The next morning Kathleen was in the middle of her morning devotions when she heard a knock on her bedroom door.

"Come in." Kathleen placed a bookmark in her Bible.

"Good morning," Papa said. He was still in his navy bathrobe and held a cup of coffee. "I know it is early, but I heard movement up here, so I thought it might be a good time for us to talk." Papa ran his finger around the rim of his coffee mug.

"Oh, yes, I am wide awake. What did you need to tell me? Is—is everything alright?" Kathleen set her Bible on the nightstand.

"Kathleen, do you remember visiting your Grandpa McKenzie's farm in Ohio when you were a young girl?" Papa sat down next to her on the bed.

Kathleen's Shaken Dreams

"A little." Kathleen looked at Papa's coffee mug that he was still fingering.

"And you remember your cousins, of course. Lindsay is nearly your age." Papa seemed as if he had something more to say but couldn't find the right words to say it.

"I remember Lindsay. She's really shy. Why?"

Papa cleared his throat. "Well, you see, dear, I had hoped things wouldn't come to this—not that a visit or move to see family would ever be undesirable, but under my present job situation—or rather the lack of a job in this case—I think it would be best for all of us if we went for an extended visit to the farm."

"Extended visit? When? I mean, for how long?" Kathleen's heart raced. What was Papa really trying to tell her?

"As soon as possible—the end of the week—New Year's Day, I'm afraid, and at this point I cannot tell you how long we will be there," Papa said gently. "You see, your mama and I have carefully calculated our savings and figured that we have enough to pay our food bills for the next six months. That excludes the bills for electricity, telephone, gas, and coal for the furnace. You see, by moving to the farm we will save the little money we have left until I am able to find another job."

"Will I miss school? What about the National Spelling Bee next spring? Surely we'll be back by then, won't we?" Kathleen's eyes filled with tears, and she quickly looked at the floor to try to hide them.

An Unforgettable Christmas

Papa put his arm around her shoulder and sighed heavily. "Kathleen, I'm afraid I cannot tell you how long we will be gone. It may only be a month. Then again, it may be a whole year. Everything depends on when I find a job." He lifted Kathleen's chin so he could look her straight in the eye. "But the one thing I promise is that I will do everything in my power to see that we return home — to Fort Wayne — as soon as possible."

"Thanks for — coming up to tell me in person. I think — I think I'll go for a walk outside now," Kathleen stammered. She ran downstairs to the back door, grabbed her coat off the hook on the wall, and stumbled through the snow banks toward her tree house.

Milk Cow, Pitchforks, and Poultry

*"My grace is sufficient for you, for my power
is made perfect in weakness."*

2 CORINTHIANS 12:9

By the time Kathleen arrived at her tree house, she was completely out of breath, but she didn't care. She just wanted to be alone—to sort everything out in her head. She climbed the rope ladder, sat on the floor, and hugged her knees to keep warm.

They were leaving New Year's Day. That meant she wouldn't be able to say good-bye to her friends at school or at church. How could they even pack so quickly?

Tears welled up in Kathleen's eyes and trickled freely down her cheeks. It was so cold out that they burned as they froze on her face, but she hardly noticed. She knew that she should be strong, but right now, it was just too much to bear. Before long the knot in her throat turned into sobs that shook her shoulders.

152

Milk Cow, Pitchforks, and Poultry

Dear God, please give me strength. The path ahead seems dark. Help me to continue to run the race of life with confidence. You promise in Your Word to never leave or forsake us — thank You that we have family to live with until Papa gets his job. But, dear Lord, I don't want to leave my home, my friends, and everything I know behind. I don't want to leave Lucy. Please help me be strong.

"Hello up there. Anybody home?" Lucy called out cheerfully from below.

Kathleen quickly brushed away her tears. She swallowed, trying her hardest to sound like nothing was wrong. "Yes, I'm here. Come on up." Her voice sounded shakier than Kathleen would have liked. She stood, straightened her coat, and worked to regain her composure before Lucy reached the top of the ladder. Kathleen could hear Lucy's carefree chatting before she even reached the tree house door.

"Your mama said I'd probably find you here. I'll tell you what, it is colder outside than —" When Lucy entered and saw Kathleen, her eyes widened. "What's wrong?" Lucy took Kathleen's hands and searched her face, her eyes full of compassion. "You've been crying."

Kathleen looked at the floor. She knew that if she was to answer right away, she would burst into tears all over again. Finally, Kathleen determined it was no use holding it in any longer. She buried her face on Lucy's shoulder and spilled her heart out in between sobs.

153

Kathleen's Shaken Dreams

"Lucy, my papa can't—can't find a job anywhere. And he says that we—we are to m-move to my grandparents' farm in Ohio by the end of the week. I asked him why we just couldn't stay here, but I'm afraid he thinks we will run out of food. I think I would almost rather starve than leave you—you are the best friend I have ever had."

Lucy put her arms around Kathleen. "This is awful. No wonder you're crying."

"Mama said that God would provide, but I never thought He would provide like this. I know I should be thankful that we have somewhere to go—there are poor people in the world who don't have anywhere to go or anyone they can turn to for help—I'm so ungrateful. This move is the most miserable thing I could ever imagine happening to me." Kathleen knew she was being dramatic, and she didn't fully mean everything she was saying—except what she said about Lucy being her best friend. On that point she was completely sincere. The thought of leaving Lucy behind in Fort Wayne was what made everything else seem so grim and foreboding.

As soon as Kathleen's sobs quieted, Lucy asked, "Do you really have to leave so soon?"

"I'm afraid so." Kathleen sniffed.

"Well, perhaps it won't be for long. Surely you'll be back in time for the National Spelling Bee. You never know, it might even be like a fun vacation—though I know I shall miss you dreadfully." Lucy paused, obviously sobered by the news. Then her

154

eyes lit up. "Didn't you tell me once you had a cousin that was almost your age?"

"I hardly know her."

"Kathleen, do you remember when I told you how hard it was for me when we moved to Fort Wayne?"

Kathleen nodded.

"I thought I'd never be happy again, but nothing could have been further from the truth. I'm sure that there will be plenty of exciting experiences ahead that you can't even imagine. After all, living on a farm without electricity and plumbing is quite unique — I always enjoy the adventure of it when we visit my grandparents' farm. And soon, you will be back home in Fort Wayne, and you can tell me all about the wonderful times you had."

Kathleen managed a weak smile. Farm life without electricity and running water would be a major adjustment. She remembered that visiting her grandparents' farm was like going back in time — with a horse and buggy rather than a car, and with oil lamps and candles instead of electric lights.

Kathleen appreciated her friend's attempt to cheer her. But no matter what Lucy said, Kathleen felt her future was growing dimmer by the second, and she could not get rid of the sick, empty feeling in the bottom of her stomach.

New Year's Eve arrived before Kathleen could scarcely draw a breath. The Meier family invited the McKenzie and the Schmitt families over for a combined

Kathleen's Shaken Dreams

New Year's Eve and farewell dinner the night before they were to leave. Mrs. Meier made a huge feast of bratwurst, sauerbraten, chicken schnitzel, German potato salad, spicy red cabbage, and a whole assortment of delicious strudels and desserts.

Kathleen forced herself to eat what was on her plate. She did not have an appetite, not only because this was her last night with her best friend, Lucy, but because Freddie sat next to her at the table. She blushed so deeply that she was afraid Dr. Schmitt would notice and think she had a fever. Just as Kathleen began to regain her composure, her papa and Mr. Meier discussed the economy and Papa's job situation and that made her lose her appetite all over again.

"I was surprised enough when the stock market crashed," said Mr. Meier, "but I don't understand why it has not gotten any better over the last few months. Things just seem to be getting worse. Why, it was just the other day that I heard Mr. Harrington was out of a job and Peter Jones too." Mr. Meier shook his head and combed his fingers through his beard.

"Things do look rather grim," said Papa, as he cut into his bratwurst. "We're just grateful to have the family farm to fall back on. Of course, things have not been easy there either. My brother says that the corn and wheat prices have dropped considerably since the Great War. But, as my father always said, 'when a man has land and livestock, he is as rich as any king'—only we may have to work a little harder than your average dignitary." Papa chuckled.

Milk Cow, Pitchforks, and Poultry

After dinner, Lucy's sister Deanna led the children in all sorts of games and fun activities. Kathleen participated in most of them and made a great effort to be her usual chipper self, but her heart was heavy. No matter how hard she tried, her eyes filled with tears whenever she thought about the move.

The dreaded time to say good-bye finally came. Kathleen's face deepened into a rosy blush when she noticed Freddie making his way across the room.

"School just won't be the same without you," he said, with an awkward look on his face. Kathleen noticed the tips of his ears were bright red. "I'm sure we'll all miss your laugh. And as for me, who will keep me on my toes during class quizzes?"

"I'm sure you will find someone to take my place. I mean, surely you'll find someone else who will be just as fun . . . just as challenging and competitive." Kathleen's cheeks burned hot and she wondered why she couldn't say what she thought in front of Freddie. She never had any trouble with anyone else.

Lucy was waiting for her in the doorway. Kathleen felt numb inside and out as Lucy gave her a big hug. "I just know you'll be back soon." Her blue eyes filled with tears. "Promise me you'll write, and don't forget to think of me often."

"Think of you! How could I forget you? And of course I'll write." Kathleen bit her lip to keep from crying. "I know I won't forget you. There's not another girl in the entire world that I like as much as you."

157

Kathleen's Shaken Dreams

Her parents were already out the door, and Kathleen knew she must leave. She gave Lucy one last hug, turned, and ran out the door, tears streaming down her cheeks.

Early the next morning, Mama shook Kathleen awake. It was still dark outside.

"Get dressed quickly, lass. Papa already has the trailer hitched up to the car, and he's started the engine to warm it up. We don't want to waste an ounce of gasoline."

Kathleen nodded and rolled over.

It was funny to hear Mama talk about wasting gasoline. She'd never thought of that before. She guessed there would be a lot of changes now. She had never worried about food on the table or gas in the car or presents for Christmas, but everything had changed—since the market crash.

Kathleen shivered as she felt through the darkness, searching for the lamp switch next to her bed. "There. I wish I could take that lamp with me, but Papa says we don't have room to bring all our belongings. I suppose the lamp wouldn't do any good on the farm, anyway." Kathleen stared at her bright yellow lampshade and shook her head.

Dear Lord, please help me—it is so hard to imagine living without electric lights or even a furnace to heat the house.

As Kathleen finished her prayer, she remembered what Lucy had said about thinking of her trip as an adventure. Suddenly the thought of Papa in a barn wearing overalls and holding a pitchfork, Mama tossing seed to the chickens with an apron full of feed, and Richard milking a cow all seemed comical. A little smile played around her lips, and she almost laughed out loud. Kathleen threw her arms up in the air and stretched. "Thank You, God, for giving me a brighter outlook!" She jumped out of bed and hurried to dress. "This may prove to be a great adventure after all."

What's ahead for Kathleen?
How will her life change?
Will she make it to Washington D.C.?

Find out in:

KATHLEEN'S UNFORGETTABLE WINTER

Book Two

ABOUT THE AUTHOR

$\mathcal{A}$uthor Tracy Leininger Craven is known for capturing the stories of real-life Christian heroines from America's past in historical fiction books. She is the author of six previous titles, including:

- **Alone Yet Not Alone**
  The Story of Barbara and Regina Leininger
- **Unfading Beauty**
  The Story of Dolley Madison
- **The Land Beyond the Setting Sun**
  The Story of Sacagawea

- **Nothing Can Separate Us**
  The Story of Nan Harper
- **A Light Kindled**
  The Story of Priscilla Mullins
- **Our Flag Was Still There**
  The Story of the Star-Spangled Banner

Tracy Leininger Craven loves history and the people whose lives have left an indelible impression on our country's heritage. She is also inspired by the testimony of God's faithfulness through seemingly impossible circumstances. Her stories of real people come alive and serve to mentor and inspire a new generation of readers.

Tracy, her husband David, and their daughters Elaina Hope and Evangelina Lilly live in the beautiful Texas Hill Country.

For more information, visit www.hisseasons.com